Kids Construction

by Ricki D. Pavlu

Copyright

Copyright 2007
Ricki D. Pavlu
"All Rights Reserved"

Library of Congress Control Number:
2007901763

ISBN:
978-0-9794055-0-1

Printed in the United States by Morris Publishing
3212 East Highway 30
Kearney, NE 68847
1-800-650-7888

Table of Contents

Acknowledgements   6
Introduction   7
Building a Relationship   9
   Give Your Children Time — "Your Time"   9
   The Felt Need of Genuine Love   14
   The Three Levels of Love   17
   Verbalize Your Love for Your Child   18
   The Three Levels of Communication   20
   Allow Children to Express Their Thoughts   23
   The Dangers of Reactive Communication   28
   Relationship Before Correction   29
   Relationship Finds the Middle Road   31
   The Replacement Factor   33
   Be One of Your Child's Best Friends   34

Building Accountability   37
   Who Is In Control Around Here?   37
   Are You a Participator, or a Spectator?   39
   Raising the Level of Responsibility   40
   Children & Entitlement   49
   To Spank or Not to Spank: That is the Question   57
   Egocentric Children   64
   Building Secure Boundaries   65
   Dealing With Conflict   66
   The One Step Rule   70
   No Pain, No Gain   71
   Empathize With Them   74
   Negative Personality Traits in Parents   75
   Boys and Girls are Different   76
   Flexibility is Not Compromise   77

Building Self-Esteem — 79
- The Provision of Emotional Support. — 79
- Give Them Respect — 83
- Meet Your Child's Emotional Needs — 86
- Keep Realistic Standards — 89
- Teach Them How to Face Failure — 90
- The "No One Likes Me" Stage — 91
- The Only One of Its Kind — 92
- Discipline to Build Self-Esteem — 93
- Verbalize Your Thoughts — 96
- Cut the Apron Strings — 97

Building a Foundation — 101
- The Mentoring Parents — Building by Example — 101
- Building a Foundation of Values — 106
- Dealing With the Emotion of Anger — 112
- It's a Heart Thing — 114

Building With Style — 117
- Being a Balanced Parent — 117
- The Overprotective Parent — 118
- The Permissive Parent — 120
- The Authoritarian Parent — 123
- The Perfectionist Parent — 125
- The Uninvolved Parent — 127
- The Balanced Parent — 130

Building Up Your Child — 131
- Planning for Your Child's Future — 131
- The Power of Parenting — 135
- Parents — The Ultimate Teachers — 135
- The Two Methods of Parenting — 138
- The Domineering Parent — 143
- Don't Put Them on a Guilt Trip — 144
- Training Up Your Child — 146

Building Character — 149
- It Takes a Parent — 149
- Building Respect for Others — 150
- Building a Positive Image of Others — 152
- What Are Your Children Being Exposed To? — 154
- Work On the Weaknesses — 155

Building a Safe Environment — **161**
    Children and a Positive Home Environment — 161
    Healthy Marriages — Healthy Children — 165
    The Dad & Mom Team — 166
    When Parents Become Nerds — 169
    Your Children & Their Friends — 170
    Kids & Freedom — 171
    Kids & Television — 173
    The Danger of Organized Sports — 174
    Concerning Sexual Matters — 176
    Dealing With Loneliness — 178

Building Your Child's Future — **181**
    Play to Their Strengths — 181
    Seeing the Big Picture — 184
    Teach Them to Look Beyond the Moment — 186
    Teach Them to Make Good Choices — 186
    Ready for Every Age Level — 189
    Socially Functioning Kids — 190
    Say Goodbye to Your Old Lifestyle — 191
    Hold Them While You Let Them Go — 192
    The Imperfect Parent — 195

Acknowledgements

      I would especially like to thank my family for giving me the experience needed to become a good parent. I treasure every moment we have shared and value each lesson we have learned together. To my wife Beverly: Thanks for all the patience, love, and guidance while completing this book. To Corrie, Jared, and Layna: Thanks for all the memories, without which this book would not have been possible. I love you all, and hope this helps you successfully build up your children!

      I would also like to give a special thanks to Mrs. Katherine Mouille for her hard work and dedication in editing this book for me. Without her literary expertise, this book would not sound as intelligible as it does. For her help, I am extremely grateful.

      I would also like to thank my son-in-law, Jonathan Walton, for the many hours of work behind the scenes, getting this work ready for publication, and Phil Moody for his careful work at editing and creating the design and layout of this book.

Introduction

Let me set the record straight from the beginning. I am not a child-rearing expert. I am not a child psychologist. I am simply a dad who has navigated through the labyrinth of decisions that a parent must make when he rears three children, two poodles, five German shepherds, a Chocolate Lab, and thirty-seven gold fish over a twenty-eight year period.

In formulating the multitude of decisions that a parent must make in rearing children, I have often felt just as I did when I would visit an unfamiliar metropolitan area. I would see the "maze" of overlapping highways and wonder if I could get through them and attain my destination without becoming hopelessly lost. This is how most parents feel as they attempt to rear children in this complex, high tech, fast-paced society that we live in today. Hopefully, this book will serve as a road map that parents can use to guide their children into fulfilling the potential that God has placed into every child's life.

By the time most parents become qualified to rear children, their children are already grown. The intent of this book is to give parents a "head-start" on child-rearing methodology before they get to the time when they look back on life and say, "I wish I would have known this when my children were first born." Important areas of child rearing such as building relationships with children, teaching accountability, and developing a child's self-esteem will be discussed in detail. Other important areas such as building the proper foundation for a child, developing positive peer pressure, and helping a child plan for his future will also be discussed.

Life offers us many opportunities, but when it comes to rearing a child, we have only one shot at it. If you are apprehensive and fear that in this world of complexity and confusion the odds are against you being a successful parent, then this book is for you.

Although this book was written with the "traditional" American family in mind, if you are a single parent or a parent in a "blended" family, do not think that you are being left out. The principles found in this book will work under any circumstances if properly applied.

Chapter 1
Building a Relationship

~

Give Your Children Time — "Your Time"

There is nothing in this world more important than our children. After God, comes family. Our children are above our church, our job, our hobbies, our friends, or anything else that fits into our list of priorities. This is not to say that these other things are not important. It is just that none of these can be superior in rank to our children. For this reason we must take time to love, listen, and build a relationship with them. Our children must know by our words and actions that they are the most important thing in our lives. The key word that demonstrates concern, love, and care in a child's mind is "time." Statistics say that the average father spends approximately 37 seconds per day in genuine interaction with his child. That is a shocking statistic, considering the time that fathers spend doing other things of lesser importance.

In this fast-paced world we live in (at this moment, while typing this, I am going 70 miles per hour on the interstate heading to a hospital in Cut-Off, Louisiana; and no, I am not driving. My wife is) it is of the essence that a parent slow down long enough to give his child his undivided attention. This requires a sacrifice on the part of the parent.

> **The average father spends approximately 37 seconds per day in genuine interaction with his child.**

It would seem that my children always wanted my attention at the most inopportune times. Just as I was rushing through the house attempting to get ready for some meeting or pastoral session with a member of my church, I would here a voice say, "Dad, you gotta minute?" Now the temptation was to answer, "Sure, next month at this time, I may have a few free minutes to give you!" In contrast to this, there were many other times when I had ample discretionary time that I could easily have shared with my children. Unfortunately, at those times it seemed that my children either had their nose in a book; their ears glued to a phone, or were typing instant messages to their friends at about 100 words per minute. I am quite certain that at those times they did not even know that I was on the same planet.

As a parent, we must realize that it is our children, and not us who "clock in" the minutes and hours of undivided attention that our children need and the "clock in" time usually begins with something like, "Dad, you gotta minute?" In other words, be there and give them the time when they need it.

A general rule in spending "quality time" with your child is to spend more time listening than talking. Save the lectures and instructions for a later date. Let your child know that he has your undivided attention. This involves putting down the newspaper, turning off the T.V., and sometimes, Heaven forbid, even letting the telephone ring without answering it.

Keep eye contact with your child and be attentive to every word that he says. When you do respond, be creative enough not to give canned answers or generalized responses. Think it out and choose your words with care. This will demonstrate to your child that he is extremely important in your life.

As a pastor, I counsel many people and prior to each counseling session I pray that the Lord will give me wisdom and guidance to say the right things and steer the individual in the right direction. I realize that the outcome of every session has the potential of changing a person's life dramatically. As a parent, I must never feel that a discussion with my child is any less important than when I counsel with a member of my church. In reality, it is far more important, because as a parent I have the power, if used properly to move my child in the direction that he will go for the rest of his life.

As the scripture in Proverbs 22:6 says:
Train up a child in the way he should go: and when he is old, he will not depart from it. (KJV)

The importance of being attentive to my child was "brought home" to me by my youngest daughter, Layna. Many times after a church service, Layna would come and attempt to ask me a question, or tell me where she is about to go to eat with her friends. Invariably there would be a number of church members surrounding me, needing to discuss various situations. Layna would wait for a pause in our conversation and then say, "Dad!" Of course, by that time another church member was already vying for my attention. She would patiently wait (there is a slight exaggeration here) for another pause and say, "Dad!" in a slightly louder voice. After a few rounds of this, she would finally say with an even louder voice, "Bro Pavlu!" It is amazing how this would get my attention every time.

Some may wonder if giving a child too much attention can adversely affect him, or even spoil him. Let me first make the disclaimer that I am not talking about improper attention, such as stifling or inordinate attention. A parent that is attentive to his child sends him the signal that he truly loves him and cares about what is happening in his life. From this point of view, a parent is unable to love his child too much or pay him too much attention. This does not spoil a child. A child is spoiled by a parent who fails to administer proper discipline, instill guiding principles and virtue in his life, and work on his character flaws.

Never try to substitute material objects and gifts in the place of the undivided attention that your child needs from you. Your unbroken, undivided attention is an expression to your child of how you care for him and love him. Love is not made of toys, guns, clothes, cars, or other gifts that a parent may give to his child. Love cannot be bought! Besides, giving a child undivided attention is considerable less expensive. This is one instance when a personal sacrifice can save you money. But I do have to be honest with you; chances are your child will ask for both your undivided attention and your money!

Time and love go hand in hand. Love is just a word floating in the ether until it is condensed into quality time spent with your child. Without this there can be no personal relationship developed between a parent and child. A parent can tell his child that he loves him, but the child is not listening to words, he is looking for evidence.

The time that a parent spends with his child is "love in action"

Let me take a moment and speak to the fathers who are reading this book. There are numerous verses in the Old and the New Testament which attest to the fact that a father should take the time to get personally connected to his children. A few of these verses are as follows:

And it shall come to pass, when your children shall say unto you, What mean ye by this service? That ye shall say, It is the sacrifice of the LORD's passover, who passed over the houses of the children of Israel in Egypt, when he smote the Egyptians, and delivered our houses. And the people bowed the head and worshipped. *(Exodus 12:26-27)*

And thou shalt shew thy son in that day, saying, This is done because of that which the LORD did unto me when I came forth out of Egypt.
(Exodus 13:8)

Hear, O Israel: The LORD our God is one LORD: And thou shalt love the LORD thy God with all thine heart, and with all thy soul, and with all thy might. And these words, which I command thee this day, shall be in thine heart: And thou shalt teach them diligently unto thy children, and shalt talk of them when thou sittest in thine house, and when thou walkest by the way, and when thou liest down, and when thou risest up.
(Deuteronomy 6:4-7)

One that ruleth well his own house, having his children in subjection with all gravity;
(1 Timothy 3:4)

And, ye fathers, provoke not your children to wrath: but bring them up in the nurture and admonition of the Lord.

(Ephesians 6:4)

A dad has a tremendous influence on both his sons and his daughters. First of all, their self-esteem greatly depends on their father taking the time to connect with them in a positive way. It is a fact that a child is always seeking his parent's approval, especially that of his father. Even when a child makes a serious mistake, he needs to hear his parent say that he loves him in spite of this mistake. A parent must remember that to forgive a child of his mistakes is not the same as condoning them.

A daughter's future relationship with men greatly depends on the relationship that she had with her dad. If it was a positive, close, and caring relationship, chances are, she will easily develop the same relationship with her

The Felt Need of Genuine Love

To create a lasting relationship with your child, you must meet his need of feeling "genuinely loved". This basic need is the same in all children. No matter what nationality, social status, race, or background, every child needs to feel loved. Now, at first, this concept may sound elementary. After all, most parents love their children. However, there is a great difference between a parent loving his child and the child feeling that his parents love him. Many parents make the mistake of assuming that their child knows that they love him; but love must be more than something assumed. Love must be communicated to the child in such a way that it is felt and has meaning to the child. Love is much more than just a warm, fuzzy, mystic feeling. Love is action. When a child knows that his parents love him, it gives him the confidence and hope he needs to face life and become victorious.

When a child does not feel genuinely loved, especially by his parents, it creates feelings of anger, anxiety, and depression. If these feelings go unchecked, they can lead to drug abuse, sexual promiscuity, and ultimately to other destructive actions: withdrawal from family and friends, and possibly even suicide.

A child is much easier to discipline and responds much better to instruction when he first feels loved. The reason for this is that love has a reciprocating effect. When a child knows that someone loves him, it tends to make him want to return that love, and thus, it becomes a natural tendency for him to please the one he loves. This is based upon a Biblical principle--THE PRINCIPLE OF FIRST LOVE. God first loved us. This is why we are able to love Him:

We love him, because he first loved us.
(1 John 4:19)

As Christians, our ability to love is based upon this principle. We do not "create" love, neither are we capable of doing so, we simply reflect the love that God has given to us. Just as much as the light from the moon does not emanate from the moon itself, so are children not capable of loving within themselves. They can only reciprocate or reflect the love they receive from their parents and others. This is why it is imperative that we give our children unconditional and unrestricted love.

The love that God has for us is unconditional. We are not able to earn it, nor do we deserve it. This is the same kind of love that we must give to our children. A child can sense insecurity and a put-on before an adult does. Thus, a genuine relationship between a parent and a child must begin with unconditional love. The need of the child must come before the need of the parent. A parent must go beyond loving the child only when the child pleases him. A parent must send the message that he is, at times, displeased or disappointed with certain aspects of his child's behavior, for which the child will be held accountable. Yet, he is still loved unconditionally.

> Unconditional love does not hold behavior as a boundry.

Unfortunately, many parents only express their love to their child when he is manifesting proper behavior. Unconditional love does not hold behavior as a boundary. Although it is proper and even essential for a parent to express his displeasure for his child's improper behavior and also to make him accountable for his actions, yet, he should at no time withhold his love from him. The parent at all times should manifest nothing else but unconditional love. This love should be manifested not only in word, but also in action. Most all parents genuinely love their children, but for some, unfortunately, their actions (at least in the eyes of the children) speak otherwise.

When a parent fails to love his child unconditionally, it causes the child to continually try to get his parent's attention and constantly seek his approval. Children have a passion for parental love and approval. The problem of low self-esteem in most adults can be traced back to this unfulfilled passion.

It is best to show your child unconditional love from a young age. However, it is never too late to begin. We serve a

God that can turn tragedy into triumph. He is able to heal any situation. It will take a little time, but showing unconditional love can and will turn any situation around.

The Three Levels of Love

People love others in three different ways. The lowest level of love is selfish love. I will define and explain this level of love in just a moment. The next level of love is reciprocating love. This occurs when one or both parties of the relationship is willing to give something to the relationship, but in return, he or she expects an equal amount out of the relationship. Many marriages and relationships sadly exist on this level of love. While counseling married couples, I have often heard statements such as, "I am willing to meet her halfway" or "this marriage should be fifty-fifty." I have always noted that they are really shocked when I tell them that their marriage giving should be one hundred-zero. That is they should individually give one hundred percent and expect nothing in return. If each of them had that attitude, it would revolutionize their marriage. This, of course leads us to the highest level of love and that is unconditional love. The Bible speaks of this level of love:

> *Husbands, love your wives, even as Christ also loved the church, and gave himself for it; That he might sanctify and cleanse it with the washing of water by the word, That he might present it to himself a glorious church, not having spot, or wrinkle, or any such thing; but that it should be holy and without blemish. So ought men to love their wives as their own bodies. He*

that loveth his wife loveth himself.
(Ephesians 5:25-28)

The Greek word used for love in these scriptures is "Agappi" which means "to give, expecting or demanding nothing in return".

Now back to selfish love. This is the level of love that all children, many teenagers, and quite a few immature adults have. The individual who loves at this level is able to receive love from others, yet not mature enough to realize that his parents have emotions and feelings also.

Many parents do not understand this concept and they take it personally when their child does not respond to or reciprocate love back to them. Children can only start at the lowest level of love and then mature to higher levels through time and experience. The issue really complicates itself when the parent loves others at a lower level, and yet, expects his spouse and child to respond at the highest level. If a parent does not understand the three levels of love, it can definitely cause a relational breakdown between the parent and the child.

Verbalize Your Love for Your Child

The old adage, "words paint a thousand pictures," certainly is true when it comes to a parent verbalizing his love for his child. Many a parent wonders in his mind, "Can I tell my child that I love him too often?" The answer to this is you can never express your love for your child too often, but you can definitely under express.

When a child is reared in a home where love is

never or very seldom verbalized, it will cause adverse effects in the child as he grows to maturity. The child will reciprocate by feeling uncomfortable in verbally expressing his love to his parents. This will lead to an awkward and tense home life. At the most, there will only be a surface relationship between the parent and child. As a result, the child will tend to withdraw from his parents. The few times they are together will result in them having very little conversation, and what little they do have will often end with misunderstandings.

A child has a deep need for love. Verbalizing the words "I love you" in conjunction with a hug will say more than buying him a toy or even a new car. Never assume that your child knows that you love him. Love must be demonstrated verbally and by action. This may sound calloused, but some parents seem to show more expressions of love to their pets than they do for their own children. Most parents feel love for their children in their heart and in their mind, but to express that love in such a way that their children interpret it as being loved, is a totally different matter. It is wonderful for parents to have a "warm fuzzy feeling" about their children, but when it is all said and done, do their children really feel loved?

> **Never assume that your child knows you love him.**

When a child is very young, he has very little verbal communication capability; therefore, we can tell him that we love him and even have a warm feeling in our heart as we say the words. But this fact alone does not mean that the child comprehends what we are saying. At this stage of the child's life, we must communicate our love to him emotionally by action: hugs and kisses. As the child grows older, he begins to connect our demonstration of love through our actions to our verbalized statements of love. This is why, as he gets older, we must continue to verbalize our love to him.

Never withhold expressions of love as a form of discipline. Love and discipline should always go hand-in-hand. As a parent issues out disciplinary action, always season it with physical and verbal expressions of love.

The Three Levels of Communication

Communication is much more than vibrating vocal cords and moving lips. There are three levels of communication that occur between a parent and his child. First, there is the "monologue command level." Next is the "mind to mind dialog level." Then there is the "heart to heart dialog level." Let us now look at these three levels of communication in some detail.

Level One Communication: The Monologue Command. Much of the time that parents spend communicating with their children is instructional time. A parent uses this level of communication to get things done. Examples are commands such as: "pick up your clothes!" "Do your homework!" "Floss your teeth!" "Don't slurp your drink!" "Stop fighting with your sister!" This kind of communication, although important in building manners, discipline, and character in a child, will not build a relationship. It is a monologue in regards to the fact that it is an issued order. Although this level of communication is a necessary part of family life, it does nothing to create a relationship between a parent and his child. It is more of a "drill sergeant" type of communication that discourages verbal response from the child. Many children interpret this level of communication as a form of "nagging." It speaks to a child's mind, but not to his heart. This level of communication alone will not create intimacy between a parent and his child.

Level Two Communication: Mind-to-Mind Dialogue. This is the level of communication that encourages a child to express the thoughts that are in his mind. It allows for a free exchange of ideas between a parent and his child. Examples of this type of communication are: "Tell me, how was your day at school?" "That's a great new hair style. How did you do it?" "What is your favorite color on a truck?" When a child is given the freedom to express his thoughts on the subject at hand, he feels as if his opinion is important and really counts. This in turn then makes him feel that he is loved and important to his parents. This also allows him to become more creative and well rounded in his thinking about social, political, and spiritual subjects of discussion.

When a child sees that his parents are listening to him, it in turn models to him the importance of listening to others, as they speak to him. As parents, we must beware of the trap of trying to squelch the ideas and concepts in our child that are not identical to ours. When a parent stops a child from expressing thoughts and opinions that are different from his, the parent is actually encouraging dishonesty in his child. Under these circumstances, a child quickly learns to keep silent or say only what his parent wants to hear on the given subject. However, this does nothing to change what the child really feels deep in his heart about the subject, whether he is correct or incorrect in his thinking.

One of the benefits of "mind-to-mind dialogue communication" is that incorrect ideas and thinking can be brought to the forefront and dealt with, instead of being kept buried in the mind of the child. Remember: to listen is not to endorse the opinion of the child. In like manner, for the child to listen is not to endorse the opinion of his parent. Proper dialogue between a parent and a child can correct a multitude of miss-aligned thoughts and concepts that are in the mind of the child.

Some parents have the bad habit of cutting off their child when he says something that they do not agree with. The tragedy of this action is that the parent will not know what strange or even dangerous ideas that his child is having until it is too late to do anything about it.

Level Three Communication: Heart-to-Heart Dialogue. This is the highest level of communication that can take place between a parent and his child. This level of communication goes beyond thoughts and ideas of the mind, and enters the area of the deeper feelings of the heart. This is the area of communication between a parent and a child that deepens their relationship and creates "bonding" between them. It is an off shoot of "level two communication," and the resulting comfort level that is produced between the parent and the child. It is usually initiated by the child. Examples: "Dad, I met this girl at school and I want to talk to you about her." "Mom did you and dad see everything eye to eye when you were dating each other?"

Tragically, some parents move straight from the "slapping hand phase" of child rearing to slapping their child's "heart". While it is important, and even vital, under the appropriate circumstances for a parent to slap his child's hand for his misdeeds, so that he may be re-directed through proper correction, yet it is emotionally fatal for a parent to slap his child's heart. Many children and young adults stopped communicating with their parents many years ago because every time they attempted to express what was deep in their hearts, their parents cut them off. This essentially was a slap to their heart. Always keep in mind that communication is the life-line between a parent and his child. Always keep it open!

Allow Children to Express Their Thoughts

Children must be given the opportunity to express what they are really feeling inside. A parent must take the time to stop what he is doing, give his undivided attention, and truly listen. First of all, this becomes strong evidence to the child that his parent truly cares about him and respects his opinions. Next, it enables a child to begin developing a proper thought process as he is encouraged to open up and express himself.

Many parents have no starting point when making an attempt to get their child's thought process in motion. The reason for this is that they have never before taken the time to sit down with their child and encouraged him to "speak out" what was truly on his mind. Once the child has opened up and expressed himself, the parent can then start at that point to direct, or redirect, the child's thoughts and ideas in the proper direction.

Encouraging a child to express what is in his mind often provokes him to ask questions. We should take advantage of these "teachable times" in our child's life. When your child asks you a question on a specific subject, it is an opportune time to mentor him on the subject at hand. Because the child has initiated the discussion, it shows that he is interested, or at least curious about the subject, and thus, receptive to teaching at that moment. These are golden moments of opportunity that may not be available at a later time. Take advantage of them.

Every child goes through a stage when it seems that every statement that comes out of his mouth is in the form of a question. I call this the "why" stage. After the parent responds to the child's question, the child counters with "why". This can become frustrating to the parent and tax his patience, but he must keep in mind that this is an opportunity to instill principles and values into his child.

As a parent, it is easy to become mind-numbed after being bombarded with a deluge of "whys." If the parent is not careful, he will follow the convenient route of responding with pat answers such as, "just because," or "I'll tell you later." He may even begin to ignore the child altogether. My associate pastor, Ricky Hardwick told me the story of a young man who was working for him. Throughout the day, as the young man worked he would continually mutter the words, "uhuh," "yeah," and "that's right." He would say these words over and over again. Finally Ricky's curiosity got the best of him and he asked this young man why he continually said those words. The young man told him that he did not realize he was doing that. Come to find out, this man had six little children with about three of them being in the "why" stage at any given time. In my mind, I thought it was a miracle the fellow could even talk at all.

If you are a father, don't underestimate the information that you can gain from your "helpmate." I sometimes think that God gave me my wife to see things that I am too stubborn to see on my own, or perhaps, the things that my male ego refuses to let me see.

    I can remember the time that my relationship with my son, Jared, had reached a critical impasse. He was at the age of sixteen and reaching a decisive time in his life. Being the strong choleric personality that I am, I became very impatient with him. Being the strong melancholy personality that he was, I kept misinterpreting the meticulous answers that he would give me on any subject that we were discussing, as insubordination and rebellion. For any question that I would challenge him with, he would begin a long monologue that I would immediately interrupt and break into by accusing him of being rebellious. This situation continued for months until the state of affairs was about to reach critical mass.

    Finally, one day, Beverly came to me in her kind, non-threatening phlegmatic way and said, "You know Rick, Jared is a high melancholy personality and needs to have the opportunity to express himself when you two are talking together." I immediately retorted, "I give him time to express himself; the problem is that he is just too rebellious to listen." She again in her phlegmatic way said, "Ricki, what I mean is that a melancholy person has to be given time to, not only begin a statement or story, but also be given time to finish it. What is happening is that, because you are choleric, you already know the end of his statement, or story, and you are cutting Jared off before he can finish saying what is in his heart. He is then interpreting this as you don't care enough to listen to what he has to say, or that he is not important enough for you to give him time to say what he is thinking." She then kindly said, "This is really not an issue of rebellion on Jared's part, or an issue of you not caring on your part, but, rather, an issue of personality conflict and impatience." She did not tell me that the impatience was on my part, but I certainly got the message. Although this really hit home to me, it was the next thing she said that really got my attention. She said, "Ricki, I am not going to tell you what to do, but if you don't do something soon, you are going to lose your relationship with your son!" That didn't just hit home, that hit like a laser guided missile targeted right between my eyes.

    I immediately got up from where I was sitting, walked to Jared's room, knocked on the door and said in a lamentable voice, "Oh Daniel, was the God you serve able to deliver you from the mouth of the lions?" He answered, "Yes, Oh great King, God sent an angel and shut up the mouth of the lions." Now this is not exactly how it happened, but the Lord really did send an angel in the form of my wife to shut up my mouth before I totally devoured my relationship with my son. What really happened is that I knocked on the door and said, "Jared, can I come in?" He responded, though I could tell with apprehension in his voice, "Sure Dad, come on in." I went into his room and sat in a chair by his bed. I then said to him, "That issue that we talked about last week, would you mind going through it again with me?" At this point Jared looked at me puzzled and to a degree, with uncertainty and said, "Sure Dad." Then he began, slowly at first, and then he got warmed up and started going into extended details. I just looked right at him with determination to keep direct eye contact with him. I said nothing; not even one interruption as he went on and on. The fact that he was not being interrupted really kicked him into high gear as he moved into the intricate detail phase of the conversation. The choleric nature in my personality wanted to stop him at every word; for sure, at every sentence, but I didn't do it. I bit my lip. I would count to ten in my mind, and then to five thousand, or so it would seem. Yet I never uttered a word. The worst part of it was that everything he was saying was so contradictory to the solution to the issue being discussed, but I was determined to give him his "say." Those words from Beverly kept echoing in my mind, "You are going to lose your relationship with your son!"

I just sat there and let him talk on and on, with my eyes glued to his, periodically nodding my head and uttering something like, "Uh huh," or saying, "I understand," while deep inside of me I was yelling, "You've got it all wrong, kid. That's not the answer to this issue!" He just kept going on and on for about eight to ten hours (it felt like that long) until he reached the end of his "State of the Pavlu Home address" and said, "That's how I see it Dad."

Now I knew that I had reached the critical moment. I knew the next words that I would say would be decisive and important. I paused and looked at him and said, "That's stupid! That's the most idiotic thing that I have ever heard in my life!" Not really, but that is what the choleric part of me wanted to say. What I really said was, "Jared, I now understand your point of view and where you are coming from, but let me point out some things that you probably didn't realize." I went into a few details and showed him a few things from a different viewpoint. After a couple of minutes of discussion on the newly revealed information, Jared said, "No problem, Dad, I can see that, I never had it explained to me that way before." What really amazed me was that it actually was the same thing I had been saying for the previous four months. Only this time, there was real genuine communication that took place between the two of us.

My relationship with Jared was restored and the lesson I learned from the experience has been great ever since. I learned that communication between a choleric and a melancholy is not only a two way street, but also that the name of the street is called "patience." At least, if you are choleric in personality as I am.

Listen to your child when he is young. He will be far more likely to listen to you when he is older.

The Dangers of Reactive Communication

The only communication that some parents have with their child is of the reactive nature. The only time that the child hears his parent speak to him is when the parent is in the corrective mode. In the parent's mind, he thinks that there is a line of communication. In the child's mind, he feels that there is no communication and he thinks of his parent as a dictator. Communication is a two-way street. It should be dialog where both parent and child are involved. Reactive communication is a monolog that is interpreted by the child as dictatorial.

A parent that is always reactive in his communication with his child may to a degree get a proper response from his child for a while, that is, while the child is young. This is due to the fear factor. But as the child grows older, he will often become rebellious, filled with anger, and sometimes even violent because of the lack of proper nurturing resulting from little or no proper communication.

The natural tendency for a parent is to give up in his attempt to properly communicate with his child. It is a lot easier for a parent to throw up his hands when communication gets tough and revert to reactive communication. But in reality, the opposite should be done. Don't stop talking until some form of mutual resolution is found to the issue that is at hand.

It is a given that there are some issues that can become quite heated and may require a cooling down period. This is a critical moment in the grand scheme of communication between a parent and his child. The child will be expecting the parent to revert to dictatorial procedures. At the same time, the parent will be greatly tempted to become dictatorial and respond to the child reactively. Don't give in to the temptation. Allow the cooling down period to have its effect, and then return to the issue, whether it is an hour or a day later.

Relationship Before Correction

If a parent fails to take care of his child's emotional needs before he corrects or punishes him, the parent will pay a great price as the child grows older. This is because a child will respond to correction through a relationship before he will respond to correction without one.

As a child reaches adolescence, if there has been no relationship developed between him and his parents, he will begin to manifest uncontrolled anger, depression, rebellion, anxiety, guilt, insecurity, or a combination of the above, depending on his personality blend. This often comes as a shock to parents. There have been many instances when I have met with parents who have made statements such as, "My boy was such a good child growing up. He was always so obedient and now all of these terrible things are coming out of him." What the parents failed to realize was that their child, while very young, was responding to correction out of fear of punishment, but there was no real relationship between the parent and child because the parent had failed to communicate unconditional love to the child. Because the child felt no love and, thus no relationship between him and his parent, he became angry, resentful, and rebellious. This child will tend to struggle with having healthy relationships with other people as he grows older. Most importantly, he will likely resist having a relationship with the Lord.

There must first be a relationship built between a

parent and his child before he will emotionally, and from his heart, accept guidance, leadership, and discipline from his parents. If there is no relationship, he may initially be obedient out of fear or other emotions, but in his heart there will be resentment and even hostility, which will later show itself in disobedience, rebellion, drug use, or other destructive actions.

When it comes to discipline, children will test their parents. Often they will not do this out of meanness or rebellion, but to see whether their parents really care for them enough to take a stand for the boundaries that they have established for their growth and maturity. They want to know if it is all talk, or if their parents really mean what they say. This is not to say that the children will like it when the parents stand firm on their rules and convictions. In fact, the children will probably get angry and fuss and fume about it. But in the end, they will develop a healthy respect and appreciation for their parents having taken a stand and not "caving in."

> **There must first be a relationship before he will emotionally accept guidance, leadership, and discipline.**

When confronted with an issue, most children are tempted to hide the truth, especially when they feel threatened by it. A parent must remember that self-preservation is a natural instinct that God has placed in all of us. Through relationship, a parent can build a safe environment wherein his child can feel unthreatened and thus be honest and tell the truth about the issue in question. This does not mean that the child will go into intricate details about the issue. In fact, most of the time a parent will have to "dig" for the needed details to get the full picture.

But in the end, if relationship is involved, the parent can feel relatively comfortable that he has heard the truth from his child.

As a child reaches maturity, the only control a parent will have over him is "relational" control. At the point of maturity, a parent will no longer have the threat, or the power of punishment. If a parent has, through the years, taken the time to build a relationship with his child, then the child upon maturity will continue to come to him for advice and will to a degree seek his council and wisdom as he navigates through life's perilous roads.

Relationship Finds the Middle Road

Parenting often requires us to make complex decisions. A parent must seek balance between being too harsh and being too lenient in dealing with his children. Every situation must be weighed by its own merits. I have learned that there are many situations that have to be adjusted by weighing out the motives of a child when he gets involved in a negative situation. When there is a good relationship between the parent and the child, it is much easier to find the middle of the road in decision-making. Not all decisions are cut and dry. Some decisions that have to be made by a parent can go either way. A good relationship between a parent and his child enables the parent to not only weigh-out the child's actions, but also his heart.

This is the relationship that our Heavenly Father has with us. We all can remember the story of Samuel going to the House of Jesse as directed by God to anoint a new king over Israel from among the sons of Jesse.

Samuel had the sons of Jesse come before him. Obviously Samuel was greatly impressed by the outward appearance and actions of Eliab, Samuel's oldest son. However, the Lord viewed Eliab from a totally different perspective:

> *But the LORD said unto Samuel, Look not on his countenance, or on the height of his stature; because I have refused him: for the LORD seeth not as man seeth; for man looketh on the outward appearance, but the LORD looketh on the heart.*
> *(1 Samuel 16:7)*

    A good relationship between a parent and a child will result in a closeness that will provide the parent with the indicators that are needed to make the proper judgment call, either in the direction of punishment, or in the direction of leniency. Every child is different. Each responds to situations according to his personality mixture. A parent must discipline his child with this fact in mind. What will work for one child, may not work for another.

    Bear in mind that the child a parent will have the most problems with, at least from the relational point of view, is the child that is similar in personality to him. Remember, the rule of thumb is that opposite personalities attract and similar personalities repel. This applies not only to dating and marriage, but also to rearing children. The next time you have to deal with your problematic child, the things that he is doing that is disgusting and angering you could be due to the fact that he is acting and thinking just like you.

The Replacement Factor

When you have to take something away form your child, always replace it with something else that is good and nurturing. Many parents do not understand the importance of this concept. When something is taken out of a child's life, it leaves a void that must be replaced. For example, if your child wants to go somewhere with the wrong company, don't just tell him he can't go. Take time out from your busy schedule and personally make the sacrifice of taking him somewhere that is appropriate to the situation at hand, and also fun by his definition.

A beautiful example of this is the way our heavenly Father has dealt with us. He took the world away from us and gave us something far better:

> *Fear not, little flock; for it is your Father's good pleasure to give you the kingdom.*
> *(Luke 12:32)*

He took something that was harmful away from us and gave us the beauty and the glory of His Kingdom in place of it.

Be One of Your Child's Best Friends

A parent should be one of his child's best friends. It is important that we, as parents, have total involvement in the life of our child. I learned this many years ago before Corrie, our first child, was born. I was preaching revival services for Lindsey Long who was at that time pastoring in Marshal, Texas. One evening, Beverly and I were invited to the Long's home. Lindsey Long ushered us into his living room. There we came upon an interesting sight. Nancy Long and her 16 year old daughter, Nancy Jr. were skipping and dancing around and around in a circle in the living room. Nancy Sr. was saying excitedly, "We've got a date." "We've got a date." Mother and daughter were so close to each other that when Nancy Jr. got her first date, it was as if the mother and daughter had the date together.

Nancy Jr. is now a mother herself and is the wife of Rick Langford, pastor of a prosperous and growing church in Lafayette, Louisiana. Nancy Long and her daughter are still "best friends."

A parent must build a relationship and close friendship with his child to the extent that the child is comfortable coming to him about any subject. There must be an open-door policy between a parent and child concerning every area of life. Nothing, absolutely nothing is taboo. If a parent does not develop a relationship in which his child is comfortable enough to ask any question he wants, he will seek answers elsewhere. Some of these areas will include humanistic teachers, non-Christian friends at school, the liberal media, and Hollywood, to mention only a few.

Some so-called "authorities" on parenting say that

parents should play the role of authority figure and overseer, and never become a close buddy or friend to their child. Other alleged "experts" on parenting proclaim just the opposite philosophy. They advocate the elimination of the authority role of a parent altogether and encourage the parent to stand on equal ground with his child and the two together become "bosom pals." In reality, both of these concepts, viewed separate and apart from one another, are wrong. Paradoxically, both concepts working together are right. The reason for this is the fact that much of parenting centers on balancing these two extremes. For example, our children should always know and respect the fact that, as parents, we are the final authority. In the role of authority figure, a parent gives instruction, guidance, and discipline. At the same time, there should be such closeness with our children, that we could be considered close friends. In the friend mode, a parent gives encouragement, praise, and unconditional love.

> **If a parent does not develop a relationship in which his child is comfortable, he will seek answers elsewhere.**

The world does a great job painting a false picture about life and its meaning. The picture painted by the world is filled with misinformation such as abortion is not murder, homosexuality is an alternate lifestyle, it is all right to have premarital sex, everybody takes drugs and that's cool. These will be the sources your child will go to if a relationship is not built with him in which he is comfortable coming to you about any subject. If he has to take his questions to those outside of your control, guess what? They will be happy to answer them for him.

Chapter 2
Building Accountability

~~

Who Is In Control Around Here?

Parents, not the children, are the ones who are supposed to be in control of a household. Some parents learn the hard way that it is absolutely essential that they maintain control of the household at all times. As a pastor, it does not take the "discerning of spirits" to look across a congregation of parents and children and know who is truly in control.

Some parents have their children well in hand, whereas others submit to every whim and desire of their children, just so their child will not "punish" them with yelling, kicking, and screaming. Other out-of-control parents are quietly, or not so quietly, screaming at their children while the children pay them absolutely no attention and go about doing whatever they want to do. I remember a question that was asked to a number of eight-year-old students. The question was, "How do you know when two adults are married to each other?" One of the eight-year-old boys responded, "That's easy, when you are in a big crowd of people, it's the two adults who are both yelling at the same kids!"

While it is important that parents be in control of their children, there is an extreme that parents can take this to. There are parents that are like Egyptian taskmasters. These parents are constantly placing unrealistic demands upon their children. They are punishment-oriented, harsh, inflexible, and are ever-daring their children to take one step out of line so they may expel their wrath on them.

On the other hand, there are those parents that allow their children to do anything. They give in to every whim and desire of their children. They are overly permissive and never provide any control or boundaries for their children to live in. Their children do what they want, when they want to, and are not held accountable for any of their actions.

Proper control is middle of the road. It is laced with mercy and discipline working hand-in-hand. This produces well-balanced children that quickly move ahead in life.

The Scripture tells us that Jesus said He had to work while it was day because the night was coming when no man could work (John 9:4). In like manner a parent must take advantage of the control that he has over his child while his child is young. As the child gets older he will lose much of that control. When a child is a baby, he, for the most part, is totally under his parent's control. When he meets his first friends, spends his first night away from home, starts pre-school, the influence of the parent begins to decline. As the child grows into his teen-age years, gets his drivers license, gets his first job, has his first date, the control of the parent diminishes even more. Finally, the day of graduation comes, then the first day of college or a job away from home. Then the wedding day, when a parent's control drops to nearly zero. Notice, I say, "Nearly zero" because we can maintain some token of control by giving out financial handouts. For example, when my oldest daughter, Corrie, was married to Jonathan, because they were both in graduate school, I told them that Beverly and I would help a little with their expenses. However, the deal was that no money would be sent through the mail. They would have to come to our home to get it. Call it a bribe if you want to, but it is amazing how well it worked. In fact, it was just like clock work. The monthly bills came due, the phone rang, and Corrie was on the other end of the line saying, "Hi Mom, Jonathan and I are coming to see you and Dad this weekend."

With the limited time that we have, we must constantly invest in building principles and values into the lives of our children, knowing that in this instance, time is not our friend. If we do not start while our children are young, when we have total control of their lives, chances are we will not be able to accomplish the task before they become teen-agers, and the control factor diminishes considerably.

Are You a Participator, or a Spectator?

Are you a parent who is participating in shaping the future of your child, or are you a parent who stands on the side-line and watches your child do as he pleases without any direction or guidance? When a parent fails to take the time or energy to build a relationship with his child, the child looses all respect for his parent and then rejects any suggestions or guidance that the parent attempts to give him. The parent, at this point, often gives up totally on giving any guidance to his child. He allows him to do what he wants, associate with whom he wants, and go wherever he wants. In essence, the parent relinquishes all power and control and becomes a spectator rather than a guiding force in the child's life.

I have met some parents who sincerely pray for their children. However, they never put any action into their prayer. They have the misconception that if they are praying, then they are exempted from putting forth the effort in building a relationship, disciplining, and building the character of their child. I have heard some parents say, "We just hope and pray that our kids turn out all right". Whereas it is vital for a Christian mom or dad to pray for their children and hope for the best, they also have the responsibility of putting some action into the child rearing process along with the hope and prayer.

The Word of God tells us in James 2:17 that faith without accompanying works is dead by itself. In other words, the Lord is telling a parent that he is to be an active participator in developing his child's future.

Raising the Level of Responsibility

Responsibility is a "process" that is transferred from a parent to his child. Children are not born with self-discipline. It is something that must be developed through time and experience. Parents do this by teaching, correcting, maintaining order, chastening, and progressively "raising the bars" on their children's level of responsibility. A wise parent makes it a goal to train his child to make wise decisions. To achieve this goal, he must give his child age appropriate freedom to make his own choices and then face the consequences of those choices, whether they are positive or negative. The parent must be willing to grant this age appropriate freedom early on in life. All young children are limited in the tasks that they can perform. As they grow from one stage to the next, a parent must learn to release his child to the next level of responsibility, while making him accountable for his actions in regards to that responsibility. The difference between an adult and a child is not years, but rather the willingness to take on responsibility.

 A parent does not place the same responsibility on an infant that he does on a toddler. When a baby is born, he lacks the ability to take on any kind of role of responsibility. When an infant cries for a bottle or has a wet diaper, it is the parent's responsibility to take care of these needs. This is the natural and proper thing to do for the child at this phase of life. All of the responsibility is on the parent, and none is on the infant.

 It is at this point that a parent must begin the process of teaching his child that living with mom and dad is not an "entitlement program". All children are born with the attitude that they have a right to get anything they want. As I said previously, it starts as little babies. If they get hungry, just cry and mommy or daddy will feed them. This does not mean at standard times such as 8:00 A.M., 12:00 P.M., and 6:00 P.M. This means they get to eat anytime they want to, even if it is 2:00 or 3:00 in the morning. If they are wet or uncomfortable, it is the same scenario. Next, they go into the pointing stage. They sit on their high chair throne, pointing and grunting at anything they want. Just like a king, they get it. As they grow older, this attitude persists. It becomes the parent's responsibility to correct this flawed concept of entitlement as their children move toward maturity.

In reality, there are only a few material things that all children are entitled to in their home. The list is actually very short. First of all is food; not necessarily filet mignons and baked potatoes. While I am on this subject let me also say that it is also not the responsibility of a parent to cater to the desires and whims of their child's palate. A parent should feel obligated to provide good nutritious meals for the child. Letting the child eat only certain junk foods that he likes is only setting him up for failure in the future.

Next on the list is clothing. This does not necessarily have to be name brands such as Tommy Hilfiger, Calvin Klein, or Abercrombie & Fitch. Then comes shelter. A private bedroom designed for a king or queen is not necessary. After all, they may have to share the room with other siblings. Next is medical provision, which, of course should be the best that can be afforded. Add to the list transportation to church and school and school supplies, and the list of necessities is complete. Anything else beyond that is a luxury, and luxuries must be earned, not doled out as welfare checks.

When a child asks for a new coloring book, a new computer, or a new car, the response of the parent should be, "What are you going to do to earn it?" This doesn't mean that a parent should treat his child as a servant or a slave, but he should begin to develop the reality that there are no "free lunches" in this life. He has to learn that in order to get rewards or luxuries in life, a person must work for them. When I use the term "earn" I am not necessarily meaning dollars given for hours worked. For example, if Johnny wants a new video game, or Mary wants a new purse, have the child earn it by vacuuming the floor or helping mom dust the furniture. Don't just hand out luxuries without the children earning them. This will only create the attitude that they are entitled to luxuries and they will go through life thinking that everyone owes them something.

Some parents make a mistake in child rearing by failing to raise the level of responsibility as the infant grows into the toddler stage. If the toddler is throwing a "fit" for a toy or for a glass of Kool-Aid, the response of the parent should be to raise the level of his responsibility for his actions and begin the first phase of developing virtues such as patience, temperance, and respect for those around him. Gradually, the responsibility that is on the parent is transferred to the child. For example, as the infant grows, the parent will introduce him to the refrigerator, and the day will eventually come when mom or dad will tell the child to open the refrigerator door and pour a glass of Kool-Aid for himself. It is not easy to transfer responsibility to a child, and most children do not buy into it immediately; after all, it is a lot easier for mom or dad to do it. As the transfer of responsibility gets closer to completion, the child discovers that if he is going to get a glass of Kool-Aid, he is going to have to get it for himself.

The transfer of responsibility from the parent to the child takes time and plenty of patience. It may also become quite messy. Just think of how many glasses of Kool-Aid have to be cleaned off the counter top and floor before the mission is accomplished. Now herein lays a great danger. As far as the parent is concerned, it is far less work to retain the responsibility and not transfer it to the child. After all, it is far easier for dad or mom to pour the Kool-Aid for their child, than it is to clean spilled Kool-Aid off the counter top and floor. However, if the transfer of responsibility is not made, it will eventually affect the child in a harmful way. A parent must be willing to exchange the convenience of the moment for the price of investing in the character of his child. The investment will then affect him for a lifetime.

I first started noticing this concept in action during church services. Some parents seemed to have outstanding control of their toddlers. This does not mean that these children did not make noise and act like children while the church service was going on, but I could tell that the parent was plainly in control of the situation. With other toddlers, just the opposite was observed. The toddler was rowdy, uncontrollable, disruptive, and was being taken in and out of the church service at his whim. This child was not given any responsibility and definitely was not being held responsible for any of his actions. He was in control, rather than his parents. In fact, he learned that if he was rowdy, he would be rewarded for his misdeeds by getting mom or dad to take him in the foyer of the church where he could then run, play, and do whatever else his little heart desired.

This same concept goes for any stage of growth in a child's life. I have watched teenagers be disrespectful to their Sunday school teachers and youth pastor. Then, if there was any attempt to call them to accountability for their action, the hard working, concerned church leader had to face the wrath of an over-protective mom, dad, or grandparent. I have watched this pattern through the years and tragically, very few of these children are living for God now that they have reached adulthood.

As a child grows and does well with the responsibilities that have been given to him, he is ready to assume new and greater responsibilities. However, parents must make certain that he is ready to climb to the next level before freeing him to do so. An event that took place

> Be willing to exchange the convenience of the moment for the price of investing in the character of the child.

between my son Jared and my youngest daughter Layna will serve to illustrate this. Jared was eight years old at the time that this happened. For a number of years, Jared had been asking me to use the riding mower to mow the grass. I would let him ride with me on the mower as I would mow. I continually told him that when he got old enough that I would let him mow alone. Finally the day arrived when I told Jared that he could mow the front lawn. I went over all of the safety instructions and reminded him again that the mower was not a toy, and that he was to be extremely careful when using it. Because Jared was so short and could barely reach the clutch, for safety reasons, I told him not to stop the mower unless I was right beside him. At that time our home was relatively new and there were no bushes or shrubs for Jared to have to maneuver around. I stayed outside while he made a few rounds, then went in the house and watched from the front window. After about fifteen minutes, Layna, who was six at the time, came to me and said, "Dad, I want to help Jared mow." I told her that she was too young to mow, but if she wanted to do something to help that she could get a glass of water and bring it out to Jared. I did not realize the potential disaster that I had just set into motion. Layna got the glass of water, ran outside and stood right in front of where Jared was mowing. I can remember this as if it were yesterday. Jared began motioning for Layna to get out of his way. Layna stood as if she was fastened to the position where she was standing. The mower got closer and closer to her. I saw all of this from the window. When it dawned on me what was happening, I sprang for the front door and ran as quickly as I could toward Layna. It seemed like everything was in slow motion: Layna with her glass of water in her hand, and Jared with his hand waving for Layna to get out of his path. All the time, the mower was getting closer and closer to Layna. At the very last moment, Layna jumped out of the way and fell to the ground, spilling the water in the process. The mower went by her missing her legs by inches. Jared looked up and saw me running toward him, realized that something was wrong, and stopped the mower. By the Hand of God, no one was hurt. I next asked Jared why he didn't stop. He simply told me that he wasn't through mowing and that I had told him, for safety reasons, not to stop the mower until he had finished. I realized at that moment that I had given Jared a responsibility that was far too great to handle at his level of maturity. It was two years later before Jared was allowed to mow again.

As children grow from one maturity stage to another, they often desire to take on more responsibility than they can handle. They will see older or more mature children doing things that they are not allowed to do and feel that their parents are holding them back, causing them to be left out of all the fun and excitement that they could be having. Often at this point they will throw the "trust" argument at their parents. I can remember Layna doing this one time when she was a young teenager. Her older sister, Corrie, was being allowed to do a number of things that Layna wanted to do. I explained to Layna that her maturity level was not adequate to match the issue at hand. Layna responded, "The problem Dad is that you just don't trust me." She was pretty shocked at the first words that came out of my mouth in response to her statement. I said,

"You're right, Layna, I don't trust you." Those words really set her back as I gave her a few moments for my statement to really sink in. I then explained to her what I meant by using an illustration. I asked, "Layna, when you were five years old, if you would have asked me to borrow the car so you could drive on the busy highway, do you think I would have let you?" She said, "No, you wouldn't have." I then explained to her why I wouldn't have let her. It was because her judgment, skill, or knowledge of danger at that age could not be trusted enough to let her drive on the busy highway. I told her that I loved her enough not to expose her to such danger. To a parent, trusting is not a matter of not trusting the heart of the child, but not trusting the experience, skill, and judgment at that present age level. I then gave her assurance that I was not trying to hold her back or punish her, but merely trying to protect her.

As your child reaches the teenage years, parental control should begin to shift towards parental trust. As a child demonstrates to his parent that he has been faithful in the areas that have been entrusted to him, the parent should reciprocate by entrusting him to even greater things. The privileges a child has and the freedom they produce should be in direct correlation to the trust that has been earned. During this time, he should be totally accountable for his actions. If he has betrayed a trust, he should be sent back to "square zero" and be made to repeat the process of building his parent's trust again.

Another way to raise a child's level of responsibility is to encourage him to become less dependent upon his parents. When a parent encourages his child to take the initiative, it causes him to think independently and take responsibility in life. This sounds strange, but some parents actually do too much for their children. A parent that does too much for his child is unconsciously causing the child to be more dependent upon him, rather than less dependent, as the child attempts to move in the direction of maturity.

Beverly is "gifted" in the area of being a "server." She will joyfully pick up after the kids, or after me, for that matter. Throughout the years, I have had to caution her about over using this gift while rearing our children. It is not easy for a server to teach responsibility because it goes against their nature. It is in their temperament to do the chores, clean the kitchen, vacuum, dust, wash, iron, and fold the clothes themselves rather than have their children help. Yet, if a parent does not teach his child the importance of taking on responsibilities, it is frightening to think of what kind of husband, wife, or employee that child will become in the future.

> **Trusting is not a matter of not trusting the child's heart.**

Reality is a great teacher when it comes to raising a young person's level of responsibility. When a young person makes a mistake or breaks a rule, he alone is responsible for doing it. This is reality! If he fails to study or waits until the last moment to do a science project, don't try to bail him out or get him off the hook. Let him face reality! The Apostle Paul spoke of reality this way to the Thessalonians: 2 Thessalonians 2:10 "that if any would not work, neither should he eat." This could easily be translated into a child's vernacular as, "If you procrastinate and fail to study, neither will you pass your exam." That's reality.

Children & Entitlement

The responsibility and character that a parent develops in his child while he is young will greatly determine the way in which he will interact with his peers in the future. When a child makes a mistake in life, a parent must teach him that he is not only responsible for that mistake, but also accountable for doing what he can to correct it. If a parent constantly bails a child out of the mess that he has made, he will begin to think that everyone he is involved with owes him something, and that he is entitled to their help. After he reaches adulthood, this attitude will greatly affect his relationship with his spouse and peers. A person with an "entitlement complex" is so obnoxious and spoiled that the people with whom he associates will question whether they want him to be a part of their future. A person with an "entitlement complex" is also unthankful and unappreciative of what others do for him. After all, he feels in his mind that it is his right and privilege to have what he wants.

Many passive parents create the attitude of entitlement in their children. This is an extremely destructive trait. When a child feels that everyone owes him something, he will demand special treatment from his family, peers, and any other authority figure in his life. When he does not get everything that he wants, he feels that he has been wronged or mistreated. When he becomes old enough to marry, he will feel that his spouse never does enough to please him. He will continuously demand unearned privileges from those around him. He will feel that he should get anything he wants, when he wants it. His needs and desires will be all that really matters.

His attitude will be that he believes he is exempted from the rules that others are required to follow.

When a child is in the infant stage, he is, and should be, under his parent's entitlement program. He neither can, nor does earn anything he receives. He is entitled to food, clothing, shelter, a dry diaper, and to having his emotional needs met. A good parent sees to it that he gets these things. The problem with entitlement begins when the child moves beyond the infant-toddler stage and Mom and Dad continue to give him anything he wants without any responsibility on his part to earn it. When this happens, he is never taught responsibility and respect for others. He is not taught to pick up his toys or to share them with other children. He is not taught to clean up his own messes because Mom or Dad is always right behind him cleaning them up. As he moves into adulthood, he still expects this from others, whether he has earned it or not.

A child with an "entitlement complex" feels that everyone in the world should focus on him. Other people only exist to meet his needs. This evolves into the feeling that he is God, or, at least, next in line to God. The sad thing about this philosophy is that people always make poor gods. A sure sign of the onset of maturity in a child is when he begins to accept the reality that he is not the center of the universe.

A child with an attitude of entitlement will very seldom use the words "thank you". His attitude about life is that everyone owes him anyway, so why should he thank someone for that which is rightfully his. Gratitude and appreciation are foreign to his way of thinking.

When children are not made accountable for their actions, they grow up to become professional blamers. They never take responsibility for any of their actions. It is always someone else's fault. It's always the bad boss, sorry spouse, mean policeman, terrible church, appalling Sunday school teacher, or incompetent pastor who is at fault; never themselves.

I am sure that most people recall the story in the Old Testament involving David's sin with Bathsheba. Nathan, the prophet of God challenged David concerning his actions. Here is the response of David:

> *And David said unto Nathan, I have sinned against the LORD. And Nathan said unto David, The LORD also hath put away thy sin; thou shalt not die.*
> *(2 Samuel 12:13)*

A person with an entitlement complex would have answered with something like this: "It's not my fault. Bathsheba should have been more careful about where she bathed. It's really her fault. Nathan, if you were really a good Prophet you would have stopped me before I sinned; so the biggest part of the fault is yours." It is far easier for a person with an "entitlement complex" to lay the blame for his mistakes on others, rather than own up to his errors in life and put forth the energy to correct them.
Some parents have the misconception that it is their responsibility to see to it that their child is happy at all times. Happiness is not part of an entitlement program. The real world does not yield happiness every moment that a person lives in it. Most of the time, it is the other way around. Job made this statement about life:

> *Yet man is born to trouble as surely as sparks fly upward.*
> *(Job 5:7)*

Problems, difficulties, and adverse situations are all part of life. A parent who is always trying to work out his child's frustrations and problems is preventing him from developing pain tolerance. This parent is unwittingly teaching his child that he is entitled to always be happy, and all he has to do is cry, pout, and throw temper tantrums and other people will always see to it that his "wants" and "desires" are met. True parental love is not giving a child everything he wants. Our society has created a generation of "takers." I am convinced that genuine parental love is giving a child everything that he "needs" but not everything that he "wants." At the same time, teaching the child to be a "giver." To this day, I have never seen a truly happy and content child who is only a "taker." A happy and balanced child not only receives from others, but also gives to others.

There have been times when parents have asked me as a pastor to intervene for their son or daughter, after their child had broken or disobeyed some law. I have seen it all the way from something as minor as a speeding ticket to vandalism of a home. I always try to explain to the parents facing these situations that the worst thing they can do in regards to helping their child, is step in and bail him out without the child paying his debt to society. This only teaches him that he will not be held accountable for his actions in the future. For example: If Johnny is busted for possession of illegal drugs, don't run to the police station and immediately bail him out. Make him feel the effect and consequences of his wrong-doing. One or two nights in jail won't kill him. I know this is a hard thing for a parent to do, but it is the right thing. A parent must make his child accountable for his actions. The scripture is very clear on this subject:

> *Be not deceived; God is not mocked: for whatsoever a man soweth, that shall he also reap. For he that soweth to his flesh shall of the flesh reap corruption; but he that soweth to the Spirit shall of the Spirit reap life everlasting.*
> *(Galatians 6:7-8)*

A parent often feels that he is obligated to break the scripture for his child's sake and bail him out so he doesn't have to reap the consequences of his actions. This also goes for the mistakes that children make in everyday living. For example, if Johnny doesn't apply himself at school, goofs off, and ends up with poor grades, a parent should not march to the school and "chew out" the teacher. If Johnny lies to his friends and they stop trusting him or having anything to do with him, don't go to the parents or pastor and tell them how bad the other kids are treating him.

When a parent places consequences on his child's actions it transfers accountability from the parent to the child. A parent cannot force his child to behave, but he can structure choices in such a way that the consequences will motivate him to make the right decisions. If the child makes a wrong decision at this juncture, his negative behavior should never be the parent's problem, but his. Yet, more often than not, a child's misbehavior becomes a problem for the parents and entire family, while the child that caused the problem remains relatively unscathed. For example, Johnny is given the responsibility of raking the leaves Mom reminds Johnny that he has three hours to get the leaves raked before the family leaves to eat supper at Grandma's house. Johnny procrastinates and does not get it done. Mom has to call Grandma and cancel the supper engagement. The entire family, including Grandma, has to suffer for Johnny's irresponsibility. What should have been done in this situation was for Mom to have transferred the consequences of Johnny's irresponsibility to Johnny. The family should have left Johnny (if he is an older teenager) home to rake the leaves while the rest of the family went to Grandma's house for supper. This would have demonstrated to Johnny that he is accountable for his actions. Johnny would have thought twice about procrastinating to do his chores in the future. In the above illustration be sure and consider the safety of the child. If the child is too young or too angry to be left at home, he should be informed that he will have to rake the leaves tomorrow and that he will have other chores added to his present responsibilities. Be sure and follow through with this the next day. Once again, the bottom line is that Johnny becomes accountable for his actions.

> **A happy and balanced child not only receives from others, but also gives to others.**

It is in a parent's nature to provide for his child. But he must not do this at the expense of failing to make his child accountable for his actions. When Johnny messes up, don't bail him out; require him to fix his own messes. Teach him that every decision that he makes in life has consequences. The consequences of a child's actions transfer the accountability for that action from the parent to the child. This, in turn, makes the problems created from the improper decisions, the child's problems, rather than the parent's problems.

There are some parents who carry their child's problems for him throughout his adolescent years. For this reason the child never learns accountability or responsibility and then his parents wonder why this is so. The parents do the fretting, worrying, and straining over the child's problems and never transfer the consequences of his incorrect decisions back to him. A child must be taught that his problems are his own; no one else's. This may sound hard and harsh, but it will go a long way in teaching responsibility and accountability to a child. If a parent does everything for his child, he is robbing him of the opportunity to become a well balanced adult.

A strong indicator of the beginning stage of maturity is when a child begins to look at a problem that he has created as his own, and then takes the responsibility to resolve it. At this point, the parent may have to give him some guidance and direction to properly resolve the problem. There are some parents who spend most of their day resolving their child's conflicts with other siblings, peers, teachers, Sunday school teachers, youth pastor, or other authority figures. However, keep in mind that it is a problem of his making. Let him play the predominant role in the resolution of it.

A mature adult identifies himself as the ultimate source of his problems and also the ultimate solution to them. Immature adults do the opposite. For them, it is always someone else's fault. Therefore, they expect someone else to resolve it. They go through life as victims, convinced that they can never be in control of their feelings and emotions. The root cause of their actions was probably a parent or grandparent who was always running a "rescue mission" to resolve their problems as they grew toward adulthood.

I have met some parents who have the attitude that discipline is synonymous with bondage. They feel that correcting their child will cause him to feel enslaved to rules and regulations. In reality, discipline, truly sets a child free. Rules in any society are usually made with a purpose in mind. For example, in the United States of America the rules of the highway state that motorists are to travel on the right side of the road, and on-coming traffic is to travel on our left side. Now we could say that these rules place us in bondage and stifle our freedom and liberty to use the entire road. In actuality, this rule gives us the freedom and relative safety to travel anywhere we want to go on any road throughout the entire mainland of the United States.

    I remember as if it were yesterday, an event that took place in my life when I was a young college student. I had just left a church event and was traveling in the east bound lane of Interstate ten. Suddenly, directly in front of me, going the wrong way on the interstate was a car that looked like it was traveling in excess of 100 miles per hour. I just had enough time to swerve out of the car's way as it flew by me. I certainly discovered that night that rules are not made to bind us, but are there for our freedom and protection.

    As I was writing this section of the book, our family poodle was kind enough to provide me with an illustration. We have a large front yard. It is approximately a one-acre area that is completely fenced in. In front of our home is a highway with a fifty-five mile per hour speed limit. Beverly let Andre' out in the yard and then became occupied on the phone. She would periodically look out the front window and check on him. A few minutes elapsed and then she suddenly called out to me in panic, "Ricki, Andre' just crawled under the fence and is at the road!" About that time a car flew by and just missed him by inches. I immediately ran to the road, grabbed him, spanked his back-side (I hope the Humane Society is not reading this), and put him back into his fenced world of bondage. At least that's probably how he viewed his world. From our perspective, it is a fenced world of safety and protection. By the way, pardon my panting; I am still trying to catch my breath.

To Spank or Not to Spank: That is the Question

The Word of God speaks much in the areas of discipline, correction, and accountability. It tells us that it is the parent's responsibility to make a child accountable for his actions. Here are only a few of the scriptures that speak on this very important subject:

> *The rod and reproof give wisdom: but a child left to himself bringeth his mother to shame.*
> *(Proverbs 29:15)*

> *Foolishness is bound in the heart of a child; but the rod of correction shall drive it far from him.*
> *(Proverbs 22:15)*

> *Chasten thy son while there is hope, and let not thy soul spare for his crying.*
> *(Proverbs 19:18)*

> *Do not withhold discipline from a child; if you punish him with the rod, he will not die.*
> *(Proverbs 23:13)*

> *Correct thy son, and he shall give thee rest; yea, he shall give delight unto thy soul.*
> *(Proverbs 29:17)*

In fact, the Word of God goes so far as to say that correcting a child is a parent's test of love:

He that spareth his rod hateth his son: but he that loveth him chasteneth him betimes.
(Proverbs 13:24)

There should be much communication involved in the process of making a child accountable for his actions. A child should know exactly why he is receiving a spanking. Spankings should be reserved for children that are toddlers up to, but not including teenagers. Spanking a child beyond the age of twelve is, at least to the child, both degrading and demoralizing. A parent's goal is for his teenage child to begin taking on the role of a young adult. For this reason, the discipline that is rendered at this age should accord with an adult form of punishment.

Astonishing as it may sound, it is far less a problem to administer discipline to a teenager than it is to a small child. Now it would seem that the case would be the opposite, but in reality there are only a few options available when a small child is concerned. However, the list of punishments is almost unlimited when it comes to a teenager. The reason for this is that a teenager has so many more privileges than a toddler or young child. A few examples of privileges that a parent can withhold to administer discipline are: use of telephones, computers, video, T.V., CD players, car, bicycle, skateboard, allowances, junk food snacks, going to sport activities, phone privileges, free time, going to social activities such as mall shopping with friends, sleeping over at a friend's house, attending parties, playing organized sports, and dating.

This list can be extended indefinitely. There are

a few exceptions that should not be used, such as wholesome food, water, shelter, and church.

Always connect the punishment with the offense. If your child brings home bad grades, then for the next six week period, his punishment is limited social activities until the next report card comes out and the proof is in the report card that he has picked up his grades. You should always require that you actually see your child's report card. If he breaks a curfew, he is grounded for one or two weeks depending on the circumstances. The grounding should include no use of the car, no buddies picking him up after school, or taking him to social activities. If he fails to take his dirty clothes to the clothes hamper or laundry room; let him go to school with whatever he can find to wear that is clean. It will probably look better than his favorite clothes anyway.

Let a child know that it is his responsibility to control his behavior; not the responsibility of his parents. At the same time let him know that it is his parent's responsibility to control the consequences of his behavior.

For a very young child, such as a toddler, punishment should be administered the moment the child makes the infraction, or at least, as close to the infraction as possible. This enables him to relate the punishment to the unacceptable behavior. For an older child, depending on the circumstances, it may be more appropriate for the parent to wait two or three days to make a decision as to the punishment to be administered for an inappropriate action. This will allow for a "cooling down period" which is sometimes needed for the parent, and other times for the child. This also gives the parent time to come up with a punishment that fits the infraction and the maturity level of the child.

One of the household chores that Layna, our

> Let a child know that it is his responsibility to control his behavior; not his parents

youngest daughter, had was to fold the clothes after they had been washed. I can remember the time when Beverly reminded Layna to fold the clothes before she left the house for a social activity with our church youth group. Due to previous church activities, the clothes for the entire family had already accumulated into quite a large pile of clothes over a couple of days. Conveniently, Layna forgot to fold them until it was time for her to dress for her get together with her friends. Beverly didn't say anything as Layna left from the house. However, when Layna got in at 11:00 P.M. that night, she walked into her bedroom to find a gigantic pile of unfolded clothes sitting in the middle of her bed, with a note saying, "You will not leave tomorrow morning until all of these clothes are folded." Needless to say, Layna spent a couple of hours folding clothes before she went to bed that night because she had something planned with her friends early the next day (about the crack of noon). The big pile of unfolded clothes on Layna's bed served as an object lesson and constant reminder of responsibility to fold the family clothes in the future.

Try to make the punishment equivalent to the severity of the infraction. For a young lady, after failing to fulfill her responsibility of folding clothes, to come in exhausted from her strenuous social life at 11 P.M. and find a mountain of clothes on her bed is punishment enough for that contravention. Layna probably had nightmares about mountains of clothes all night long.

If there is a major infraction, such as out-right rebellion or drug abuse, make the punishment equivalent to the violation. For example, if your child is caught with drugs, it would not be too severe to take vehicle privileges away from him for six months, while totally severing his social relationship with any friends that might be "drug buddies" indefinitely.

I have had parents come to me on numerous occasions and tell me that they know that their teenager is too old to spank and that they just don't know how to discipline him. On each occurrence, I would wonder what planet this parent came from. In a moment, even with the limited knowledge that I had of their teenager, I could think of numerous interests and areas of passion that their child enjoyed that would have served as a perfect thing to withhold from them for a specified time in order to discipline them. Always remember, whatever is a passion or an intense interest to a teenager is a weapon in the hands of a disciplining parent.

Now back to the subject of spanking, in regards to toddlers and young children. Proverbs 22:15 was not meant to be only for children of the Old Testament, but is applicable and also relevant to children of the 21st century. Notice what it says:

Foolishness is bound in the heart of a child; but the rod of correction shall drive it far from him.
(Proverbs 22:15)

The Word of God doesn't soft petal the issue of rebellion in children. It uses the term "the rod of correction" and it means just that. It doesn't use the popular term of "time out" that so many parents try to substitute in the place of spanking today. A parent must face this reality, there are some things in a young child that cannot be talked, reasoned, or timed out. Only "the rod of correction" (spanking) will deal with rebellion in a young child. However, spankings should not become a "catch all" punishment, but should be confined to areas of rebellion, outright-defiance, willful disobedience, and areas of danger. Do not use the threat of a spanking for every mistake, rowdy action, or miss-step that a child makes. A parent who does this will soon discover that it will soon loose effect and the child will simply begin to ignore it. In other words, the threat of a spanking should be replaced with the certainty of a spanking if he persists in the inappropriate action. Follow your words with action, not with more idle threats.

When properly applied, spankings break a child's strong and stubborn will, but not his spirit. A spanking should always be administered in private and never in public. A parent must always be certain that he is in control of his emotions before he spanks his child. There is a proper way to administer a spanking to a child. It is essential that a parent be in total control of his emotions throughout the process of the spanking being administered. It is always wrong for a parent to administer a spanking to his child when he is angry or emotionally out of control. Never spank a child when you are in a rage or cannot control your passions. A parent can usually tell when his child's will is broken by the actions that the child manifests. If the child reacts in anger or manifests an attitude of stubbornness, his will is not broken. If he is spanked, and after a few minutes of crying or whimpering, he reacts with a sincere attitude of apology (not necessarily in word, but in action, mind-set, and, and mannerism), then his will is broken.

Some parents tend to under-spank their child which results in his will not being broken. Other parents tend to over-spank their child, which creates other problems.

A parent with this problem spanks his child for any and every reason. This results in desensitizing the child to correction and discipline, which eventually results in resentment toward authority figures in his life. This resentment eventually turns into deep seated rebellion in his heart.

Once a child's will is broken and he, in his childlike way apologizes for his mistake, it becomes a parent's responsibility to receive his apology, show him affection, and reward him with a hug. This in turn shows him two important things: First, "If I do wrong, I am going to get a spanking and be punished for it." Second, "if I do right, I am going to get hugs, kisses, and/or other rewards for it." Often, a parent will feel guilty when he has to correct his child. It is in a parent's nature to do good things for his child. For this reason correction can cause a confusing, contradictory emotion within a parent. It is important that the parent clarifies the emotion that is within him, or he will tend to under-correct his child. He may even choose to not correct the child at all.

Let us identify the Biblical principle that explains the emotion that a parent should feel when he has to correct his child. It is found recorded in the book of Hebrews.

And ye have forgotten the exhortation which speaketh unto you as unto children, My son, despise not thou the chastening of the Lord, nor faint when thou art rebuked of him: For whom the Lord loveth he chasteneth, and scourgeth every son whom he receiveth. If ye endure chastening, God dealeth with you as with sons; for what son is he whom the father chasteneth not?
(Hebrews 12:5-7)

Notice carefully that the emotion manifested by the

Lord when he chastises his children is not one of anger, hatred, or guilt. Rather, it is the emotion of love. I found that using the word "love" when I corrected my three children served a two-fold purpose. First of all, it kept my emotions focused properly. In other words, I didn't let anger control me as I corrected my children, nor did I feel guilty during or after the punishment was administered. Next, it explained to my children the importance of why they were being corrected. Daddy cared for them and loved them enough to call them to accountability for their inappropriate actions. For example, I would make statements such as, "I love you enough to say no!" "I love you enough to not let you go to that place!" "I love you enough to make you accountable for what you have done!"

Egocentric Children

If a parent does not teach his child responsibility, he stands to create an egocentric attitude within him. An egocentric child thinks that his desires and feelings are all that count. This child has little or no regard for anyone else's feelings. When an adult does not respect the feelings of his spouse or peers, the problem can usually be traced to a lack of training in the areas of responsibility and accountability during his younger years. The goal of a parent should always be to impart responsibility into the life of his child. A part of that responsibility is to be sensitive to and respect the feelings of those around him.

Teaching a child responsibility makes him accountable for his time, talents, actions, and attitude. It makes him aware of the fact that his life and all that it entails is something that God has entrusted him with. He becomes aware that he alone will ultimately decide what he does with it. Children who are taught responsibility learn to take control of their lives. Through the realization that they are in control of and accountable for their actions, they discover that they are free to choose the way they are going to live their lives. They can choose to live a selfish, self-centered, and inconsiderate life, or they can live a selfless, altruistic, unselfish life. By making the right choice, the potential and possibilities of their lives become limitless.

We live in a society today that is tragically out of control. Many adults live with a "victim mentality." They inadvertently pass this on to their children. These people feel that everything should be done for them and they are not to be held accountable for their decisions and actions.

Building Secure Boundaries

The other day, I was having my oil changed by a mechanic that is a member of my church. Al brought me to the back of his shop and showed me a bulldog that was on a chain. The dog was barking and exhibiting extreme excitement. Al told me that he had tried to let the dog have more freedom by letting him stay off the chain. However, when the dog was released to do whatever he wanted, he became very insecure up to the point that he went and hid inside of his doghouse. The same is true with children. Too much freedom without properly defined boundaries makes children insecure.

Boundaries in a child's life are like rules in a game. Try to play monopoly, chess, or some other game without any rules. First of all, it would be extremely frustrating. Next it would create insecurity because a person would never know whether he was winning or losing. This is exactly the emotional feelings that are inside of an undisciplined child.

Dealing With Conflict

Conflict is inevitable between a parent and his child. This is a world of complexity and there will be misunderstandings. Arguments, mix-ups, misinterpretations, and mistakes made by the parent or the child need not end on a negative tone. Strong relational bonds are created when a parent resolves a conflict with his child through communication and expressions of forgiveness under the umbrella of unconditional love. Never leave your child with the feeling that you have not forgiven him. This will create feelings of guilt and low self-esteem in him.

Remember, forgiveness is a two-way street. There are times when a parent will make a mistake in judgment. At these times, it is important for the parent to ask his child to forgive him. This is not a display of weakness, but rather a demonstration of how to ask for forgiveness. This is a skill which many, both young and old, lack.

Most parents are introduced to conflict the first time they attempt to set a limit on their toddler. Every child, without exception responds to a limit with anger. Depending on the personality of the child, some will respond with more anger than others. The truth remains, when a child first hears the word "no," he will deal with his newly set limit as if it were his mortal enemy. He will resist it! He will fight against it! His sweet little demure will turn to rage. I am convinced that the first time a parent introduces a limit to a toddler; that event becomes a decisive moment in the child's life. If the parent remains firm, realizing the fact that anger is to be expected from the child, then the child will begin the first step of learning that there are limits and boundaries in life that he must live within. On the other hand, if the parent regresses, it will teach the child that a limit can be circumvented if he throws a big enough fit. Tragically, this is also the first step in demonstrating to a child that he can manipulate others by his negative actions and improper attitudes.

All children will test their parents and challenge their authority at some point. A child will see how far he can step outside of the boundaries that are set for him. He will become angry, critical, disrespectful, and even lie to get his way. He will then selfishly justify his reason for stepping outside of his boundaries. The only thing that will put him back within his boundaries is discipline.

This goes for children of all ages. I remember when Jared was a toddler close to two years old. Beverly and I were visiting some friends of ours in North Louisiana. It was approaching time for us to go to bed. Beverly looked at Jared and said, "It is time for Mommy to put you to bed." Jared immediately responded in as firm a voice as he could find for a toddler and said, "No!" Beverly then approached the couch where Jared was sitting and said, "Jared, let Mommy take you to bed." Jared immediately stiffened up and said in an even louder voice, "No!" This was the moment that I decided to step into the situation. I looked at Jared and said, "Jared, I am not going to let you go to bed until you tell your momma that you are sorry!" He looked strait into my face and said, "No!" I looked right back at him and said, "Jared, you are not leaving this couch until you tell your momma you are sorry, even if it takes all night!" At this point, I told Beverly to leave us alone in the living room. I then settled down for the duration. About every fifteen minutes, I would ask Jared if he wanted to tell his mommy that he was sorry. Each

time he would respond, "No!" This went on for about two hours. Periodically Jared's eyes would droop, and I would say, "Wake up, Jared. You are not going to bed until you tell your mommy that you are sorry!" At about 2:00 A.M. Beverly came and whispered in my ear and said, "Ricki, I don't think he understands what you are wanting him to do." I told her that beyond a shadow of a doubt, he knew exactly what he was doing. I then sent her out of the room again. After about thirty more minutes, with his eyes half closed, Jared looked at me and said, "Dad, I torry." He immediately proceeded to hop off of the couch. I quickly stopped him and said, "Jared, that is not what I said you would have to do to go to bed. You will have to go into the other room and tell your mother that you are sorry." He immediately hopped off the couch and ran into the bedroom. He went up to his mother and said, "Mommy, I torry" and then climbed into bed and fell asleep.
This was a defining moment in Jared's life. It was a battle between his will and that of his parents. If Jared had won this battle, it would have been even harder to win the next battle with him.

     Not only does discipline make a child accountable for his actions, but it also re-establishes boundaries and re-defines limits in his life. This is the only way that a child will build respect for his parents and others. It will also develop the virtues of patience and temperance in his life. Notice, this same concept is portrayed in the scripture involving our relationship with our Heavenly Father:

> *Furthermore we have had fathers of our flesh which corrected us, and we gave them reverence: shall we not much rather be in subjection unto the Father of spirits, and live? For they verily for a few days chastened us after their own pleasure; but he for our profit, that we might*

be partakers of his holiness. Now no chastening for the present seemeth to be joyous, but grievous: nevertheless afterward it yieldeth the peaceable fruit of righteousness unto them which are exercised thereby.
(Hebrews 12:9-11)

This scripture tells us that the end result of discipline in our lives is the "peaceable fruit of righteousness". It would seem that everyone wants the end-product of righteousness but no one wants the process of chastening to get it.

Maintain total control of your child in important, essential areas. All other areas are negotiable. For example, untidy rooms, improper eating habits (within reason), loud music (Gospel), and faddy clothes (as long as it is modest) fall within the perimeter of tolerance. However, zero-tolerance must be exercised in the areas of alcohol, drugs, pre-marital sex, associating with the wrong friends, breaking the law, and lying. By giving leeway in the negotiable areas, a parent emphasizes the essential, non-negotiable areas. This helps the child clearly recognize these important areas and the fact that he is never to cross the boundary and step into those areas. In other words, choose your battles wisely. Learn to distinguish between a mountain and a mole-hill. Save your energy and influence to challenge the mountains that are in your child's life. Don't be nit-picky with your child, and then when the time comes that you have to cry "wolf," your child will respond to the danger.

Let me take a moment and touch on the subject of blended families. I don't mean to sound negative, but if you are a parent in a blended family, the problems and confusion that are going to take place in your home are magnified a hundred-fold in comparison to those of a traditional family. The pecking order for siblings of a different parent family can become chaotic and confusing. On top of that, the questions of which parent has the authority to correct which child and to what extent must be answered. Add to this the subconscious thoughts that are in each parent of the "blended family" as to whether his or her child is getting fair and impartial treatment, and you have a ready-made scenario for child rearing problems.

Now, be honest with yourself. You didn't ask for your first marriage to end in divorce. Perhaps you were the innocent party, the victim in the broken marriage. Now, also be real with yourself. This does not change the fact that your "child rearing scenario" will be more complicated than the "same parent scenario" of child rearing. Yet it can be done, and done well, with the help of God, and discipline and determination on the part of you and your spouse.

The One Step Rule

When it comes to discipline, all a parent has to do is stay one step ahead of the child. I call this the "one-step rule." When a child breaks a rule of the household, all a parent has to do is stay one step ahead of the child and punish him. If he breaks the rule ten times, all the parent does is stay one step ahead of him and punish him on each occurrence. If the child breaks the rule a thousand times, stay one step ahead of him on each occurrence and punish him. In reality, even a strong willed child will usually get tired of being punished consistently for the same misbehavior after a few attempts to see if his parents will cave. If the child persists in disobeying the same rule, it is probably time to intensify the punishment.

The greatest cause of a child failing to develop discipline and self-control in his life is a parent who does not have enough discipline and self control to stay one step ahead of his child, making him accountable for his actions. If a parent will follow the one-step rule; discipline will beget discipline. If the parent has enough discipline to stay one step ahead of the child, it will eventually create self-discipline in the child's life.

No Pain, No Gain

Discipline is always painful to a child. In fact, if there is no pain then it is not truly discipline. There is a vast difference between the pain of discipline and the harm that comes from not providing for a child's needs. Proper discipline, though painful, is always constructive. It builds character, virtue, and values in a child. Abuse, on the other hand, is always destructive. It causes physical and psychological damage to a child.

There is an old cliché that says "no pain, no gain." Many parents hesitate to discipline their children in the attempt to spare them pain. What they fail to realize is that a little pain up front, will prevent untold pain in a child's future. Some parents get the misconceived idea that disciplinary pain is harmful, when in reality it is the other way around. Notice the following verse of scripture:

> *Now no chastening for the present seemeth to be joyous, but grievous: nevertheless afterward it yieldeth the peaceable fruit of righteousness unto them which are exercised thereby.*
> *(Hebrews 12:11)*

This scripture tells us that the pain of chastening

will produce the "peaceable fruit of righteousness." The pain of discipline is the policeman on the street that keeps the peace and upholds the law by keeping evil men within boundaries through the threat of painful retribution. In like manner, the threat of disciplinary pain in a child's life tends to keep him within safe boundaries. This creates self-discipline in him, which becomes an asset as the child reaches adulthood.

It is a normal feeling for a parent to dislike the responsibility of inflicting disciplinary pain upon his child. A parent's obligation to mete out disciplinary pain upon his child is also painful to the parent. Yet, at the same time, it represents the kind of love that God has for his children. The Word of God is emphatic on this subject:

> *And ye have forgotten the exhortation which speaketh unto you as unto children, My son, despise not thou the chastening of the Lord, nor faint when thou art rebuked of him: For whom the Lord loveth he chasteneth, and scourgeth every son whom he receiveth. If ye endure chastening, God dealeth with you as with sons; for what son is he whom the father chasteneth not?*
>
> *(Hebrews 12:5-7)*

Plant the "seed of disciplinary pain" in a child and it will produce a "harvest of character" in his future. A parent must teach his child to make pain his friend, instead of his enemy. A child will do his chores when the pain of not doing them becomes greater than the pain of doing them. A child will develop people relation skills when the pain of having no friends becomes greater than the pain of changing his behavioral attitudes. A child will do his homework when the pain of losing social privileges becomes greater than the pain of doing the homework. This same scenario will continue after a child has entered adulthood. An adult will learn to control his spending when the pain of bankruptcy becomes greater than the pain of not purchasing everything he wants. He will develop good spousal relations when the pain of potential divorce becomes greater than the pain of not having his way.

Some parents, unknowingly, try to circumvent God's Word. The scripture says:

Be not deceived; God is not mocked: for whatsoever a man soweth, that shall he also reap.
(Galations 6:7)

This is the "law of the harvest." It says that a person will reap what he sows. In other words, there is a natural consequence for a person's actions in this life. The "law of the harvest" makes a child naturally accountable for his own actions and decisions. For example, Johnny is given a five dollar allowance for the week. He blows it all at the beginning of the week, and then sees something he wants to buy in the middle of the week. He reaps the natural consequence of poor stewardship by having to do without the thing he wants. However, if his parents step in and purchase the thing he wants after he has blown his allowance, they are by-passing the natural consequences of his unwise decision and making him unaccountable for his action.

Empathize With Them

Although children bring problems upon themselves by making incorrect decisions in life, a parent should still express sympathy for them while keeping them accountable for their actions. Romans 12:15 tells us to "Rejoice with them that do rejoice, and weep with them that weep." This scripture applies not only to fellow church members or strangers on the street, but it also applies to our children.

When a parent sets a limit on his child and the child chooses to break it, the parent must not only stand by the limit that was set, but also empathize for the resulting loss that the child faces for his inappropriate actions. For example, if a parent were to tell his daughter that she is only allowed to go out with her friends once per weekend, and she approaches the parent to request a second social event, the response of the parent should be to remind her of her limits. Next he should empathize with her. It should sound something like this: "Dad, there is a brand new store opening in the mall and all of my buddies are going this afternoon. Can I go with them?" "Mary, remember the discussion we had last week? You know that this is your last week-end before mid-term exams and I told you to plan only one social event for this week-end. You chose to use it last night to be with your friends." "Yes, but Dad, I didn't know about this neat new store opening until my friends told me about it last night. Couldn't I still go and study extra hard when I get back?" "Mary, I know it's really hard to miss the grand opening of the new store. I know how I feel when I have to miss some event due to other commitments that I have made.

It's the pits isn't it? But look at it this way, you'll have something to look forward to next week-end."

Empathizing with a child won't make him happy about his situation. In fact, he may even express frustration or anger. But when it is all said and done, he will know that his parent cared enough to try and identify with his pain.

Negative Personality Traits in Parents

Every man, woman, and child on the face of this earth has one of four dominant personalities. Although everyone will have a mixture of the four, one will dominate in his or her life. These four personalities have been given names. They are as follows: Choleric, Phlegmatic, Melancholy, and Sanguine. Space would not allow me to have a thorough discussion on personalities; however there are many good books that have been written on this important subject. One that I would highly recommend is Personality Plus by Florence Litteaur. I would like to take a moment and present the negative extremes that are found in each one of these personalities, in regards to parenting.

First, let me deal with the Choleric personality, not because it is more important than the other personalities, but, because it is my personality. The Choleric tends to be a dictator. He will over-use corporal punishment because he has "drill sergeant" tendencies. He will tend to be insensitive to the needs of his children.

Next is the Phlegmatic personality. He tends to be too permissive because he does not like to deal with issues. He will be hesitant to correct his child or call him to accountability. He usually prefers to overlook his child's mistakes.

The Melancholy parent tends to deal with his children according to his mood swings. He demands perfection out of them and gives them little room for mistakes. He does not allow them to act like children by demanding too much order out of their lives. He focuses too deeply on discipline.

Last is the Sanguine personality. He tends to be too self-centered to see the needs of his children. He is oblivious to the importance of meeting their emotional needs. He fails to observe the weaknesses of his children until they magnify to the point of being out of hand; then he over-reacts in correcting them.

When a parent identifies his negative personality traits, it is far easier to correct them. A good parent will work on his weaknesses; thus becoming a better parent.

Boys and Girls are Different

Perhaps at one time or another you have heard an elderly person contrast the difference between little boys and little girls by saying, "Little girls are made of sugar and spice and everything nice, and little boys are made of snips and snails and puppy dogs tails." There is much truth in this statement. In fact, boys are totally different from little girls. They talk, act, think, and react to stimuli in totally different ways.

Some parents have the misconceived idea that little boys and little girls are only different in their physical makeup. They fail to realize that they also have a completely different physiological makeup. A little girl will respond to a situation in one way, whereas a little boy will respond to the same situation in a totally different way. A good example of this can be seen when young boys and young girls are playing outdoors. If the group were to encounter a frog, the girls will tend to be repulsed by it and walk away from it. The little boys will tend to attempt to catch it and then if they succeed, they will usually proceed to chase the little girls with it.

A parent must not make the mistake of expecting or demanding the same response from his son as he does from his daughter, and vise versa.

Flexibility is Not Compromise

There is a vast difference between flexibility and compromise. Compromise is giving ground in areas that will do untold damage to the future of a child. Flexibility, on the other hand, is the ability of a parent to recognize that there are times when rules have to be stretched to meet a need in a child's life.

A good example of this can be found in James (name has changed). James is a young man of about fourteen years of age attending the church that I pastor. He became infatuated with a young lady whom I'll call Mary. She was also about the same age as James. Mary came from a family whose father, sisters, and brother were all highly involved in drugs. When James's father heard about the developing relationship between James and Mary, he had to take a stand and made the rule that James would not be involved with or associate with Mary anymore. This, of course, devastated James, who, in turn, became embittered and eventually rebelled by associating with Mary behind his father's back.

One thing led to another and James was eventually caught with drugs at school. His father took him home and tried to reason with him. James became enraged and busted the door of his bedroom off its hinges. The father of James next called for the youth pastor of our church to come to his house and council with James. The father was hoping that the youth pastor could get control of the situation and perhaps talk some sense into James. What happened next is really amazing. The youth pastor did talk to James for quite some time. He then came out of the room where he had been talking to James and told the dad these shocking words, "You have left James with no hope for the future." He explained to the dad the feelings of hopelessness that were in the heart and mind of James. He then encouraged James' father to give his son "hope without compromise."

> **Inconsistency is more detrimental to a child than being too lenient or too firm with him.**

After much discussion between the father and the youth pastor, they came upon this decision. James was told that if he would do what was right for the next three years, and if Mary would live for God and live right as validated by her pastor, that James would be released to date Mary at that time. The end result was that the attitude of James immediately changed and he began to do better. His father's willingness to be flexible, and yet, not compromise in a crucial area of life probably saved James.

On the other hand, a parent must be consistent with his discipline. Don't let a child break a rule and get away with it one day, and break the same rule the next day and be punished for it. Inconsistency is more detrimental to a child than being too lenient or too firm with him.

Chapter 3
Building Self-Esteem

The Provision of Emotional Support.

A parent must provide emotional protection for his child as he goes through the traumatic stages of maturing into an adult. This requires him to be keenly observant to any emotional change in his child. I am not necessarily talking about the constant up-and-down response that occurs in every child's life. What I am speaking of here is major mood swings caused by situations in a child's life that play havoc with his self-esteem.

For example, when a child says, "I feel as if I am ugly." Don't ignore this as just a passing whim. Take time to ask for details and dig for the root of what really caused this attitude. Correct his thinking and give him strong moral and emotional support. This goes for any kind of negative thought or feeling that the child is having about himself. It is absolutely vital to the emotional well being of the child to trace these feelings to the source of the thoughts and eliminate them. I can remember the time that Layna came home and told her mother that her best friend told her that she dressed ugly. This statement from her friend really worked on Layna's self-esteem. Beverly quickly went to work on helping Layna trace down the source of her friend's statement. Come to find out, a young man in the church in whom her best friend was interested, had begun to show Layna quite a bit of attention. Beverly explained to Layna that her friend was feeling threatened by the situation and the negative statement about the way Layna dressed was her response to it. Once Layna was armed with this knowledge, she not only had her self-esteem restored, but she also understood why her friend reacted the way she did. She then became careful in her actions toward the young man, thus preserving the friendship.

Self-esteem does not come from winning a soccer game or from doing some activity exceptionally well. Winning an event will cause a child to feel good for a short time, but it will not create any lasting feelings of self-worth. True self-esteem comes to a child when he has a sense of belonging. When a child truly feels that he belongs to a loving, caring family, it creates a sense of security and well-being that gives way to positive feelings of self-worth. When a child feels that he is important to his family, he is liberated to use his personal giftedness and unique talents to contribute something back to his family, church, friends, and community.

Often, when a child misbehaves, he is responding to an important personal need that is not being met in his life. He may be responding to something in his past that has caused bitterness, resentment, frustration, or anger. We must hold him accountable for his actions, but at the same time seek to find, and to meet the overlooked need that initially caused his misbehavior.

Do not fall prey to the emotional intensity of children. This is especially true concerning teenagers. The teenage years of a child are characterized by roller-coaster emotions. This is normal. A teenager can be excited and laughing at one moment, and depressed and sad the next. Rapid changes are taking place in a teenager's life. Nearly every teenager is sensitive to change and their moods change to match the changing circumstances.

I can still remember the time, a few years back, when Layna came home from school in a happy mood. She was laughing and excited when she stepped into her room. The next instant she came running out of her room crying and very upset. This dramatic mood shift occurred when she looked in her dresser mirror and discovered that a fever blister was forming on her lower lip. This new discovery was combined with the fact that she had school pictures to take the next day.

At a time like this, don't try to over-rule your child's emotions with a lecture on your knowledge and wisdom about life's issues. Also, never try to match your emotions with theirs, because they can always take their emotions to a higher level than yours. As a parent, I will admit that it is easy to be sucked into the vortex of a child's emotional whirlwind. When this occurs, it usually ends with a shouting match between the parent and the child. The parent winds up pulling rank, shutting the child up or sending him to his room. This, of course, does not resolve the emotional trauma that is taking place inside of the child.

When a child is emotionally distraught, he is not looking for logical answers or lectures. Amazingly, he is not even looking for a solution, because emotionally there is no solution. For example, you can say, "Oh honey, go ahead and have your picture taken tomorrow. The photographer can always touch it up in his studio." However, a solution to the problem is really not what a child is looking for, or needing, at such times as this. What they are really wanting is for their parents to listen; I mean, really listen-- to the point that they feel that you comprehend their pain. In other words, they want to feel understood, which is nearly impossible for a parent to do with a teenager.

Always remember that at times of emotional turmoil, a teenager is incapable of truly hearing what a parent is saying, no matter how loud or professional the answer may be. Therefore, what a parent is saying is not as important as the supportive feelings being conveyed to the child during the crisis. Once the child calms down, which teenagers do every now and then, he will be able to hear and comprehend a logical solution that you may offer to resolve the problem.

A parent must exercise intense patience with his teenage child. When the child explodes in a mass confusion of words (I am not talking about profane, vulgar, or disrespectful words), do not follow him down the hall or into his room attempting to force him into a verbal confrontation. He is not ready for that. Rather, wait twenty or thirty minutes, allowing time for him to calm down, then ask him to allow you to talk to him. Most of the time, he will respond in a positive manner. For example, if Mary runs into the house from school and says something like, "I have zits everywhere, I am so ugly, I hate myself, I am never going back to school again, in fact, I am never leaving my room again!" Don't chase her down the hall trying to convince her that she is beautiful. Don't try to get her to logically talk about the situation.

First of all, she won't listen because she is incapable of doing that at that moment. Next, which is probably the most important point; your actions tell her that you really don't understand what she is going through. This is why teenagers so often say, "Mom (Or Dad), you really don't understand what I am going through." The parent usually responds with something like: "Let me tell you what I had to go through at your age. I had to walk three miles to school and I only had one pair of shoes to last the entire school year." At this point they are not ready for a history lesson about how bad it was in the "old days." Children live in the moment. They have no comprehension about time lines or about the "pre-historic" days.

This was brought to my attention in a vivid way, when Jared was about six years old. I was telling him about some of the things that I did when I was a boy about his age. As I paused to say something else, he suddenly looked at me and said, "Dad, were you a little boy when the Civil War began or had you already grown up?"

Give Them Respect

To build self-esteem, a child must feel that he is respected by his parents. Do not treat your child as a possession, but as a gift from God. Notice what the scripture in Psalms has to say on this subject:

> *Behold, children are a gift of the LORD; the fruit of the womb is a reward. Like arrows in the hand of a warrior, so are the children of one's youth. How blessed is the man whose quiver is full of them; they shall not be ashamed, when they speak with their enemies in the gate.*
> *(Psalm 127:3-5, NAS)*

A child learns by example. If a parent does not respect his child, how can the child be expected to respect others? When a child is respected by his parents, it also builds their relationship. This translates later into the child treating others with dignity and respect. Respect is given to a child by creating clear boundaries for him to live by; then enforcing them with consistency. If a child steps outside of the clear cut boundaries that are set by his parents, he must face the consequences. This tells a child that his parents care enough about him and respect him enough to make him accountable for his actions.

At the same time, a parent must set limits on himself in regards to invading his child's privacy. For example, knock on your child's door before you enter his room. Don't have the attitude that your child's room belongs to you (although it does), or that you are paying for the electricity for his room (although you are), so this gives you the right to step into his room anytime that you want to. Don't read his diary or his e-mails unless you have reason to suspect something is amiss. If there are justified reasons for suspicion of drug use or some other deep form of misconduct, don't leave a stone unturned. Although you want to show respect to your child, at the same time, you don't want to be naive. Your child may scream "unfair" with this form of treatment, but serious misconduct demands serious action from you. In this area, a parent must juggle two balls at one time. He must make the child feel that he has the freedom to make his own decisions in life, while also keeping a firm hand on the decisions that the child makes.

Another way to let a child know that you respect him is to listen to him when he is attempting to hold a conversation with you. Most conversations between a parent and his child are short circuited in the first few moments of the attempted transaction. Because children lack in basic communication skills, adults tend to be impatient. They fail to give children time to find proper words to use to develop statements that are critical for dialog to take place. When a parent cuts his child off in conversation, the child may interpret that he is not important to the parent. A parent must realize that body language is a very important part of communication. Improper use of body language suggests impatience, lack of concern, or misunderstanding.

Another reason parents tend to cut children off in a conversation is because their maturity level is superior to that of the child. In most situations, the parent already knows what his child is going to say on a given subject. At least, he assumes he knows what his child is going to say. For this reason he unconsciously cuts his child's words off before he is finished. The child is never given the opportunity to reciprocate his feelings on the subject at hand. This makes a child feel disrespected and quickly erodes a relationship. On the other hand, when a parent intently listens to his child and gives him time to communicate what he is thinking, the child feels that he is respected by his parents and in turn his self-esteem is enhanced.

> **If the parent does not respect the child, how can the child respect anyone?**

Of course, there are exceptions to what I have just stated. There are times when a child will loose control of his temper and say things that are inappropriate. There are other times when he will throw a temper tantrum because of selfishness or not getting what he wants. There will be times when a child will interrupt a conversation taking place between other people. In all of these situations, stop the child and let him know that his interruption or behavior is unacceptable. Require him to calm down before he is allowed to resume talking again. Sometimes even forcing an apology may be appropriate.

A parent should also respect his child enough to, "allow him to be his own man." Many parents are uninformed in the area of personality mixtures. For this reason they make the mistake of expecting or even demanding that their children act and respond to various situations in life just as they would. This lack of respect for the personality make-up of their child stifles his potential and creates havoc in the parent-child relationship as the child becomes old enough to begin making decisions on his own.

Meet Your Child's Emotional Needs

When a parent begins to see the first signs of uncontrolled anger, rebellion, anxiety, depression, insecurity, or other negative attitudes, these are the tell-tale signs that a child's emotional needs are not being met. It is the parent's responsibility, not the child's teacher's, Sunday school teacher's, or youth pastor's responsibility to be on the lookout for these signs. Just as being aware of early cancer symptoms go a long way in the cure, so it is with developing emotional well being in a child.

The more a child's emotional needs are being met, the more positive he will feel about himself. Meeting a child's emotional needs is not to be interpreted as giving in to his every whim. In reality, it is just the opposite. Taking the time to teach a child responsibility and virtue demonstrates to the child that the parent truly cares for him. This creates an emotionally safe environment for the child.

The child will then feel more secure and positive about himself. Only when a child feels good about himself, can a parent expect him to excel and reach his potential.

Young adults who were properly nurtured as children tend toward high self-esteem. They enter into adulthood feeling that life has been good to them. They then have the attitude that they want to give something back to life. This moves them in the direction of becoming emotionally healthy, productive Christian citizens, spouses, and parents.

A child that is under-nurtured tends toward low self-esteem. He enters into adulthood fearing life. Any change of circumstances at home or in the work arena tends to intimidate him. He will have a propensity to struggle with relationships because of the emotional baggage he carries.

A child who is over-nurtured tends to expect everything in life to be handed to him. This person will usually have an entitlement mentality throughout life. He will feel that he should not have to work for anything. He will also feel that he is not accountable for any of his actions. After all, someone will always bail him out of his problems just like mom or dad did when he was young. He will be a pessimist, blaming everyone and everything when his needs are not met. He will always want to have his way, even if he has to step on others to get it. Notice what Solomon had to say about this:

The rod and reproof give wisdom, but a child who gets his own way brings shame to his mother.
(Proverbs 29:15, NAS)

This is a negative world. Rear your child in an environment of optimism. When a parent expresses to his child that he has confidence in him, it sets up an environment for him to do his very best and then releases him to excel. Expect the best from him. This within itself provides the dynamics to move him in a positive direction.

Teach your child to have a positive attitude about himself. Explain to him that he must first love himself so that he can, in turn, love others:

> *For all the law is fulfilled in one word, even in this; Thou shalt love thy neighbour as thyself.*
> *(Galations 5:14)*

Next, teach your child to have a positive attitude toward life:

> *Finally, brethren, whatsoever things are true, whatsoever things are honest, whatsoever things are just, whatsoever things are pure, whatsoever things are lovely, whatsoever things are of good report; if there be any virtue, and if there be any praise, think on these things.*
> *(Philippians 4:8)*

Then, teach your child to have a positive attitude toward others. Remind him that God created every person on the face of this earth with potential, and when God does something, He doesn't do shoddy work:

> *I will praise thee; for I am fearfully and wonderfully made: marvellous are thy works; and that my soul knoweth right well.*
> *(Psalm 139:14)*

The natural and spiritual level of success that a

child will attain in life is determined by the level of self-esteem that a parent instills in him. If a parent wants his child to have a better chance of attaining a deep relationship with God, excelling in his career, developing quality relationships, and maintaining emotional health, he must invest time into building self esteem. Ephesians 6:4 admonishes parents to "bring up" their children in the nurture and admonition of the Lord. Other words that could be used in place of "bring up" are to "build up" or to "strengthen." It is always a parent's responsibility to lift up his child's emotional well-being and never tear it down.

Keep Realistic Standards

Some children feel that they can never do enough to please their mom or dad. No matter what they do, they never receive approval from their parents. Even when they do some project or job well, their parents let them know that they could have done it better. There is never positive affirmation, only negative criticism. These children eventually become insecure or angry because they feel incompetent and incomplete.

It is all right, and even good, to have high standards for your children, as long as they know that you have unconditional love for them. Encourage them to strive for higher levels of efficiency, but at the same time compliment them for what they have already achieved, no matter what level they have attained.

There is a major difference between a parent placing a high expectation upon his child to be an achiever and a parent encouraging his child to do the very best at whatever he attempts in life. Placing unrealistic standards for a child to be an achiever in all areas of life puts undue pressure upon him. He then correlates achievement with self-esteem. When he does not achieve, or fails in some area, his self-esteem diminishes. A child who is encouraged to learn from his mistakes and feels no undue pressure to perform enjoys life with his self-esteem intact.

Teach Them How to Face Failure

In the secular world, success is defined as always winning and being on top of whatever a person endeavors to do. Granted, winning is part of the formula for success. However, another part of the formula is learning to handle losing in a positive way. Failure can move a child forward in life if a parent will teach him to use it as a stepping stone, rather than seeing it as an obstacle or stumbling block.

Many parents spend quite a bit of time teaching their child how to succeed, but never teach him how to gain value out of failure. The reality is that not everyone is going to take first place in the foot race. Not everyone is going to hit a home run. Not everyone is going to be first string on the football team. Not everyone is going to make the top grade in class. This is certain, and a parent must teach his child how to cope with this reality. I am in no way implying that a parent teach his child to be a second-rate person. Rather, teach him to search out his strengths and weaknesses, then play to those strengths and excel in those areas.

The "No One Likes Me" Stage

Most children, at some point in their life, go through the "no one likes me" stage. This usually happens when a child feels that he has nothing to offer anyone. This feeling usually causes him to retreat from his friends and peers, isolating himself from social interaction. In turn, his peers interpret his isolation as him being snobby or socially inept. They will then tend to leave him alone and have nothing to do with him. This action on the part of his peers provides credence to his original feelings that no one likes him. He becomes convinced that what he is thinking about himself is true. It is easy to see how this vicious form of low self-esteem can quickly escalate into a serious matter.

In this situation, a parent must help his child build up his image of himself. Let him know that God has given him unique and personal gifts that can be used to help others. These gifts may be things as simple as a friendly smile, listening ear, word of encouragement, helping hand, or an ability to help others organize their life. As a parent, let him know that it is his responsibility to take these gifts to his friends and peers. Also, let him know that they will not come to him and ask for the use of his talents at first. For example, if he has a great smile, convince him to spend a day or two smiling at everyone he sees. He will be amazed at the number of friendships this will open to him. At the same time, prepare him for the reality that not everyone will respond appropriately to his smiles. There will always be the bullies and smart-alecs that will see him smiling and retort with such statements as: "Who are you smiling at?" or "I am going to take that smirk and push it down your throat!" However, there will be far more that will respond appropriately. The end result will create many avenues and opportunities for developing friendships.

Showing a child his giftedness and teaching him to share it with others increases self-esteem, manners, propriety, respect, and wisdom.

The Only One of Its Kind

Children must be made to recognize that they were uniquely created by God. Society has given children a misconception about real life. It portrays success as being a great athlete, model, or movie star. Yet 99.99% of all children do not fit into those categories. This creates unrealistic, self-imposed expectations on children that they will not be able to live up to.

It is the responsibility of a parent to emphasize to his child that he is a distinctive creation of God. He is fearfully and wonderfully made by God Himself. The Master Architect and Designer of the entire universe created him in his uniqueness. He is different from every one else on the face of this earth. This will go against the grain of peer pressure that is trying to tell a child that he should look, act, and dress like the in-crowd. However, by letting the child know that he is one of a kind from a positive view point will help to neutralize the negative view point of his peers. If a parent can get his child to grasp this concept of uniqueness, then just as a one of a kind painting by a famous artist creates value, so will a child's knowledge of his uniqueness create positive self-esteem.

When we build self-esteem in our children, we lay a foundation for character building. A child that feels good about himself and feels self-worth tends to live up to that image. If he feels he has value to God, himself, and others; he will tend to move his life in the positive direction of building his character. On the other hand, if a child has low self-esteem and feels that he is worthless, he tends to sabotage his life by constantly making improper decisions. His negative self-image becomes a "self-fulfilling prophesy."

Discipline to Build Self-Esteem

Proper correction is vital if your child is going to be in an environment that is conducive to building self-esteem. In my opinion, firm correction is essential in a child's proper upbringing. However, discipline should never be administered at the expense of belittling or degrading a child.

A sure way to depreciate an older child's self-esteem is to discipline him in front of his friends. A parent's goal should be to call his child to accountability for his actions, not to traumatize or embarrass him. Older children feel that a parental trust has been violated when a parent disciplines him in front of his peers. Some parents correct their children in public to give the message that they are the "boss" in their family. A parent must be mature enough to avoid this type of self-indulgent temptation. After all, which is more important: to look good in front of peers or protect the self-esteem of the child? The personality mixture of some children is such that if a parent corrects the child in public, he may be so humiliated and embarrassed that the trauma of the experience may follow him the rest of his life.

Words such as "You are stupid" or "You are so

ugly," should never come out of the mouth of a parent in public or private. Children are extremely sensitive and their emotional nature is fragile. This is why child abuse and molestation is so devastating. It affects a child emotionally to the point that it takes a lifetime for many to recover. The sad tragedy is that some never recover. A similar situation occurs when a parent gives his child sharp unmerited criticism or makes careless, belittling comments that degrade him. Never make mocking comments of derision or disparagement about your child's abilities, performance, or looks. Remember, God didn't call you to tear your child down, but to "build him up."

All children have emotional needs that must be met. To merely respond or react to a child's behavior is treating the outer symptoms of a child's needs and not going to the inner source. Correction should involve both areas. Let the child know that there will always be punishment for unacceptable behavior and that he is accountable for his actions. At the same time make certain that you are communicating your love to him in such a way or in as many ways as are necessary for him to know for certain that you do love him. Thus, you are meeting his emotional needs.

When a parent corrects his child, setting limits for his actions or life style, it will usually anger the child. He may express this anger in an open and obvious way, or he may simply act or look disappointed. This is when the parent is most vulnerable to giving in or backing up on the punishment that has been rendered. It is important for a parent to recognize these feelings are normal under such circumstances. It is only natural for a parent to not want to see his child unhappy or disappointed. It is vital at this juncture for a parent to not give in to personal feelings, but do what is best for his child. To stand firm on right decisions of correction and discipline raises a child to a higher level of accountability and demonstrates to him that he is responsible for every action that he takes in life.

Discipline should always be pro-active; never reactive. When a parent disciplines his child out of anger it is really not discipline, but child abuse. I am an advocate of corporal punishment because it is a Biblical principle. This does not mean that I in any way endorse child abuse. Child abuse has become a plague in our society that we must constantly war against on all fronts. If you are having a problem in this area, you need to stop what you are doing and seek help immediately. These kinds of actions will negatively affect your child for the rest of his life. This book was not written to address this type of disorder. This is a serious problem that must be dealt with, but is outside the scope of this book. However, as the old adage goes, "Don't throw the baby out with the bath water!" Corporal punishment plays a vital role in bringing discipline and balance to a child's life. Neglecting to deal with a child's strong behavioral improprieties can have devastating effects that can ruin a child's life and sabotage his future by playing havoc on his self-esteem as he grows older.

> **When a parent disciplines out of anger, it is really not discipline, but child abuse.**

Verbalize Your Thoughts

A parent must never assume that his child knows what he thinks about him. Just as a parent must verbalize his love for his child, so must he also verbalize his thoughts about him. Tell him that you are proud of him. Your child needs to know that you think he is honest, hardworking, dedicated, loving, committed, and giving. He needs to hear you say it in your own words. Use every descriptive word that you possibly can.

If you never tell your child what you think of him, he will grow up with a big question mark about himself. He will constantly be on a quest for approval. If he does not get it in verbal form, he will eventually become frustrated and relinquish all attempts at bettering himself. Instead of having an attitude of excellence, he will have an attitude of failure and worthlessness.

An interesting fact that goes along with this scenario is found in the method that cults use to recruit new members. Statistics reveal that the thing that attracts most young people to "cults" is not the doctrine they teach, but the positive acceptance the prospective new members receive from the cult's membership. This fact demonstrates the vital importance of parents verbalizing compliments about the character and talents of their children.

Cut the Apron Strings

It is imperative that a parent move his child toward independence. There is nothing more pathetic than a "dependant" young adult who looks to his mom and dad for every decision in life. They tell him what to eat, where to go, whom to associate with, where to move, whom to date, when to get up, and when to go to bed. He is an adult, but they are still treating him as if he were five years old.

Have you ever met a dependant young adult that has high self-esteem? I'm sure you haven't. A sure way to destroy a child's self-esteem is to refuse to "cut the apron strings" as he grows toward a higher maturity level.

Most of the time, dependency weakness in a young adult originates from a parent refusing to allow his child to reach for maturity as he grows older. This causes the child to be emotionally dwarfed as he enters his young adult years. Very often, this person will continue to live with his parents, not marry, and submit to every decision his parents make for his life.

An excellent way to create independence in a child's life is to offer him choices. For example, when it comes time to order at a restaurant, allow your child to pick his entrée (within an acceptable price range). The only disclaimer that you place upon him is that he has to eat what he picks. When it comes to buying clothes, let him make his choice out of three or four items that you have pre-sorted. Within certain boundaries that are pre-set, let him create his own agenda for week-end activities. Even let him pick his own friends, as long as they fall into the proper Spiritual and Biblical criteria. In each of these areas let him know that he is the one who is making the decision. As he grows older, broaden his horizon by giving him more and more choices. As you see his maturity level increase resulting in him making good and appropriate choices in life, disassociate yourself more and more from his decision making by giving him more control of them.

Cutting the apron strings is much like teaching a child how to drive. At first, the parent chooses some lonely dirt road to begin the driving lessons. The parent's hand practically stays on the steering wheel with the child's. The parent tells him when to shift, when to take his foot off the brake, when to accelerate, where to turn, and how far to go. As the child gains experience, the parent tells him less and less until the parent's responsibility is only fine tuning the child's decisions as he moves into being an experienced driver.

By letting a child make more and more decisions in life, the parent is building the child's confidence, as well as strengthening his ability to steer through the obstacles of life. This is called independence.

Another area of independence in which a parent must release his child is the area of problem solving. When a child comes to a parent with a problem, even if the answer is obvious, don't give it to him immediately. Help him think his own way through to the solution. Ask him to verbalize the problem. This helps him to see the issue clearly. Then have him verbalize one are more possible solutions. Steer him in the direction of the best solution by asking him other questions and giving him input at the proper time. Once he has the solution to his problem fixed in his mind, let him know that he came up with the answer himself and that all you did was act as a sounding board. This will greatly build his confidence in his ability to solve problems in the future.

Some parents make a terrible mistake in this area of their child's life. When their child gets into trouble, they are always bailing him out and taking care of his problems. Often they will blame everyone else for his problems. By doing this they make him totally unaccountable for his actions. When he makes a mistake, does wrong, or gets into trouble, along comes mom or dad with red emergency lights flashing, pushing everyone out of the way, and whisking their little darling back into the safety of the synthetic, secure little world that they have created for him. Once again they are in control of his life. Unfortunately, he is totally dependant on them and is unaccountable for any of his actions.

It is very important to build accountability in your child during these moments. In most cases, if a number of people are having trouble with your child, and your child is declaring innocense, something is amiss. Also, if most of the children that are your child's age are isolating your child, chances are, your child has done something to warrant those actions. Use these times not only to show your child that you are in their corner, but to teach them that they must be accountable for every action in life.

Chapter 4
Building a Foundation

The Mentoring Parents — Building by Example

A child receives his first lesson on principles, virtue, and character in the home. He sees how Dad and Mom think, live, and reacts to various situations in life. For this reason, the lesson he learns can either be good or bad. Therefore, it is a parent's responsibility to not only teach character, but to model it. Children tend to look up to adults and emulate them. This is the reason children love to dress in adult's clothes and shoes. I can still vividly remember the many times that Layna, as a four year old, would climb on the brick ledge in front of our fire place in our living room. She would then act as if she was on the platform of our church building, put a little plastic pipe in her hand and imitate Paula, one of the singers in our church. She did a great job of imitating the motions and actions of this singer. This phase of Layna's life continued for about three years. During this three year period, Paula had two children. During the time Paula was obviously "expecting," Layna would do her singing with a pillow stuck under her shirt. When the baby was born, out would go the pillow. As a parent, we must always remember that our children will tend to imitate our actions when they are younger and our lifestyle when they are older. This should be a sobering thought for any parent.

We must build a proper foundation for our children. One of the ways of building a foundation is to mentor our children. The old adage is true, "We must lead by example." We must be an example in every action of our life. They must see us pray. They must see us genuinely love our spouse. They must see us demonstrate honor, virtue, and character. They must see us faithfully go to church and financially support it with our tithes and offerings.

While it is good to seek to improve your parenting techniques, it is only superficial if you are not improving your own personal life. Focus on yourself as a parent and not just on your techniques of parenting. As a parent, you must model honesty, virtue, character, discipline, steadfastness, gentleness, kindness, forgiveness, and love, to name a few. The best way to improve situations and weaknesses in the lives of your children is to first improve yourself.

In the equation of "parent and child rearing," you are the only part of the equation over which you have total control. We all hope and pray that our child-rearing techniques will cause our children to turn out all right, but there will always be that gray area of uncertainty as to the end results. Yet, you are always in control of how you will turn out. Improve yourself and there is a certainty that the example you leave your children will be worthy for them to follow.

When I was a little boy of about the age of four, my dad was an electrician by trade. Day in and day out, I would live in the imaginary world of being an "electrician." This was all I ever saw my dad do and whether he realized it or not, he was mentoring me to become an "electrician." I would play my made up game of "Ricki the Electrician" for hours with my plastic screwdriver and my imaginary wire and equipment. I can remember the day that one of the appliances in our household was being repaired. The repairman took some of the internal components out of the appliance to bring to his repair shop. Unknowingly to me, he told my mom that he also took the plug off the end of the electrical cord to make certain that the appliance would not be accidentally plugged in. After the repairman left our house, I decided to inspect his work. I saw the electric cord without the plug and immediately discerned the problem, being the "great electrician" that I was. I took the end of the cord with the loose wires and pushed them into the receptacle next to the appliance. Instantly, blue and red flames spouted from the receptacle. Loud explosive sounds accompanied by black and gray smoke came from the appliance. My mom ran into the kitchen and almost ran into me running out of the kitchen. Needless to say, my career as an "electrician" was short lived.

Just a few months after the "Electrician Episode," my dad had a career change. The U.S. Post Office employed him as a mail carrier. From that moment on, at least during my younger years of life, I could be found in our house delivering imaginary mail to every covey hole that I could create out of drawers, shoe boxes, or whatever would transform into a mail box. My entire household found that being a postman was a much safer imaginary occupation for me.

As a rule, children tend to follow the example of their parents. If a parent is faithful to the Word of God, to supporting his Church, and to prayer; the children will usually follow the example. As a pastor, I have noted that most of the time, children and young people will follow the example that their parents have set. If the parents are faithful to Church, usually the children will be after they are old enough to be on their own. I have especially noted this when it comes to tithing and other financial support rendered to the Church. If the parents have been faithful tithers, usually their children are just as faithful as they mature and leave home. Their parents built a proper foundation of stewardship into their lives. They led by example and it was only natural for their children to follow. Unfortunately, if the parents were not faithful with their tithes and other financial support to their church, then most of the time, their children were just as unfaithful at maturity. Once again the children followed the example of their parents.

> **Children reared by parents with a good marriage tend to have good marriages themselves.**

Another area where parents set examples for their children to follow is in the way they conduct themselves in their marriage. This is why it is so important that parents maintain a great marriage. From a parent's modeling as a husband or wife, his/her son or daughter is learning how to act when they mature and become a husband or wife. A great marriage should engage in mutual love, trust, respect, open communication, and romance.

Don't think that your children aren't watching your actions as a husband or wife. They see far more than you see. Adults are usually blinded by their personal biases. They are in the middle of the arena. The children are in the bleachers watching the action. Children reared by parents that have a good marriage tend to have good marriages themselves. Sadly, children that are reared by parents that have bad marriages tend to repeat their parents problems in their own marriage. Check out our national statistics in this area and you will find this to be true. On a positive note, if you were reared in a home with a bad or broken marriage, with the help of the Lord, you don't have to repeat your parent's mistakes. The Lord can empower you to rise above statistics.

When a husband or wife says, "This divorce only involves my spouse and me," who are they kidding? The ones most affected are their children. They will be affected for a lifetime. For this reason, it is vital that a parent identify his marital weaknesses and work on them. Many problems in life tend to flow from on generation to the next. They are passed from parent to child. The way to break the generational curse is for a parent to ask God to help him identify his character flaws that are affecting his marriage. Once identified, he must ask the Lord to forgive him and to help him overcome these weaknesses in his life. Don't think that this is an easy task that will be accomplished overnight. This will take much time and hard work. God will help any person who asks for help, but this does not negate the fact that the individual involved must still do his part.

Remember, your children are watching what you do much more than they are listening to what you say. When we model good character and excellence in our marriages, our children will usually follow suit. At least, the statistical odds of them having a good marriage will tilt in their favor.

Building a Foundation of Values

In some ancient pagan religions, custom demanded that a parent offer his child to various gods such as a "sun god" or a "moon god." Today, a parent would be appalled at the thought of taking the life of his son or daughter in this manner. Yet, his lack of responsibility in building a foundation of values in his child has the same affect, at least in the spiritual sense.

Two generations ago, people had a consensus of agreement on the rights and wrongs of life. Values and virtues were well defined. Although the "Builder Generation" did not always follow what they believed as to what was right or wrong, at least they had an agreed definition

In some ancient pagan religions, custom demanded that a parent offer his child to various gods such as a "sun god" or a "moon god." Today, a parent would be appalled at the thought of taking the life of his son or daughter in this manner. Yet, his lack of responsibility in building a foundation of values in his child has the same affect, at least in the spiritual sense.

Two generations ago, people had a consensus of agreement on the rights and wrongs of life. Values and virtues were well defined. Although the "Builder Generation" did not always follow what they believed as to what was right or wrong, at least they had an agreed definition on the values of life. In other words, they had some absolutes that they believed in.

All of this changed with the "Baby Boomer Generation," which is my generation. Today many parents are not taking the time to pass values on to their children because they don't live them in their own lives. They are too busy, selfishly living their lives, making money and spending it (most of the time over-spending it with credit cards) to realize their responsibility in molding values in the hearts and lives of their children. I feel this is the reason that most young people in our society are increasingly unable to define what is right or wrong. Absolutes and values have turned into a shady gray area of fuzziness. The situation has now deteriorated to the point that the world tells us that there are no rights or wrongs, only opinions. Anyone who defines something as sinful or wrong is a bigoted, judgmental person. For example, they say abortion is no longer murder but a mother's choice. Homosexuality is no longer an abomination in the sight of God, but simply an alternate life style. Sex outside of the marriage bond is not adultery or fornication; it is rather a live-in partnership. We have lived to see the day when a man who held the highest office in the United States of America, the Presidency, could lie under oath, lie to the people of the United States, commit perjury, and continue being President until his term was finished.

A similar situation occurred a few thousand years ago as recorded in the Bible. David was king over Israel at that time. David had become a very elderly man when this incident took place. He had a son named Adonijah. Notice what the scripture says about this man:

> *Then Adonijah the son of Haggith exalted himself, saying, "I will be king"; and he prepared for himself chariots and horsemen, and fifty men to run before him. And his father had not rebuked him at any time by saying, "Why have you done so?" He was also very good-looking. His mother had borne him after Absalom.*
> *(1 Kings 1:5-6)*

David had never built a foundation of values in the life of Adonijah. Perhaps David was too busy ruling Israel to take the time to rule his own household. But whatever the case, Adonijah grew up with no restraints or self-control imposed on his life. As you can see from the scripture, he later tried to usurp the throne from his own father.

Our children are being reared today in the midst of a social environment with no absolutes. If they are to gain the true definitions of virtues, principles, and character, it must be taught to them in the home by Godly parents. It is our responsibility, not the governments or public school's, to teach our children how to think properly when it comes to virtues and principles. One way to do this is for a parent to share his feelings about situations and decisions that he is facing with his children. This not only goes a long way in developing a relationship with them, but it also teaches them the proper thought process involved in coming to the proper conclusions in various situations and circumstances that life will pose. Then, when they are faced with a similar set of circumstances, they will be armed with the knowledge to think properly and come to an appropriate conclusion.

Some parents have the philosophy of giving their child the freedom to make up his own mind about what he wants to believe after exposing him to various ideas and view points. Yet, the scripture is adamant that a parent's obligation is to "train up a child in the way he is to go." This "training up of a child" includes spiritual, ethical, and moral philosophies. I strongly question whether a parent with this loose type of philosophy has any bed-rock beliefs whatsoever.

In the "training up of a child" there are some areas that are non-negotiable. As long as the child is living in his parent's home he should be required to attend church and youth events. In rearing all three of our children, Beverly and I have never been approached with the request of missing church or church related activities by any of our children. From our actions and lifestyle, our kids knew that going to church was a bed-rock rule of our household that could not, and would not be broken. On various occasions I have been asked by parents whether they should let their child make their own decision as to whether they would attend church. I have responded to these parents with questions of my own. They go something like this: If your child asked for the choice of playing on the Interstate highway, would you give him the choice? If your child asked for the choice of going to school or not, would you give him that choice? Which is more important to you, your child's safety, his education, or his soul?

While we are on the subject of church attendance, let me say that almost every parent will, at some point, hear his child say, "I don't want to go to church." The first thought that a parent usually thinks after he hears this is, "Oh no, that which I have greatly feared is come upon me. My child is already moving in the direction of becoming the world's greatest heathen." The parent will then respond to his child, "You will go to church." The child will then respond, "Why?" The parent will answer, "Because I say you have to and I'm bigger than you!" This concludes the discussion, but it doesn't deal with the issue of why the child did not want to go to church in the first place. It may be something as simple as the child is sitting next to a bully in Sunday school who is always picking on him. Sometimes it is simply that a teenager would prefer to sleep-in, rather than get up and get dressed for a church service. At other times, it is that the Sunday school class or the Children's Church is boring to the child.

A mother in the church that I pastor had three

young daughters. One day she discovered that one of her daughters did not want to go to Children's Church. She did something that most mothers would do. She brought it to my attention. She then did something that most mothers would not do. She told me that she was willing to volunteer her services in any way that would help improve Children's Church. We held a meeting with the Children's Church teachers. It was discovered that the problem was simply that there was too much age difference between the children attending Children's Church to hold all of their attention. This caring mother took the younger children, started a separate Children's Church for them and completely resolved the problem.

    A great way for a parent to coax his child into becoming more attentive in Sunday school is to take the time to ask him what his Sunday school lesson was about. Most children love to play the role of a teacher and will often go into great detail about what they were taught during the Sunday school lesson. As the week progresses, a parent can then ask his child to explain to him how he is applying the lesson to his life. This sounds very time consuming, and guess what, it is! Yet, isn't it amazing how a parent will take the time to make sure his child is learning the alphabet and his multiplication tables, but will send his child to Sunday school and never take the time to see if his child is learning the truly important things in life that will last throughout eternity.

    A few months ago I had a dream. Now most of my dreams come from eating too much pizza, but every now and then I dream that I am preaching a message which actually turns out to be pretty good, or I wake up with a pretty good sermon thought. On this particular night I dreamed this statement: "I would really enjoy my dream world, but reality keeps getting in the way." There are some parents that try to change the "reality" of life to match the desires and wants of their children, instead of requiring their children to change their life and attitude to match true reality. As a pastor, I have dealt with parents who try to convince me to change the minds of Sunday school teachers, Children's church leaders, the youth pastor, or anyone else who was in a position of authority over their child. Instead of requiring his child to develop disciplines in his life, the parent would rather demand that the rest of the world change to match his son's flawed paradigm. This reminds me of the story of the mother who was sitting in the bleachers looking over a military parade field, watching a battalion of soldiers marching. She spotted her son marching and said to the person next to her, "Isn't my son wonderful, out of all those soldiers marching out there, he is the only one marching in step!"

We must pass on the "moral baton" to our children. The scripture tells us to "run the race that is set before us" (Hebrews 12:1). Yet, if we fail to pass the baton on to our children, we have missed one of the major purposes in being a parent.

Solomon, the "wise man" of the Old Testament had this to say on the subject:

He that is slow to anger is better than the mighty; and he that ruleth his spirit than he that taketh a city.
(Proverbs 16:32)

He that hath no rule over his own spirit is like a city that is broken down, and without walls.
(Proverbs 25:28)

Be not hasty in thy spirit to be angry: for anger resteth in the bosom of fools.
(Ecclesiastes 7:9)

Dealing With the Emotion of Anger

Uncontrolled anger can destroy a home or relationship. I feel that the reason there is so much violence and abuse in our country today is the result of parents who have not taken the responsibility of managing their children's emotion of anger in the home.

One of the ways of managing a child's anger is by illustrating the difference between "positive anger" and "negative anger." Positive anger is a righteous indignation against something that is wrong or evil and results in that which is constructive and helpful. Negative anger is "out-of-control-anger" that results in that which is destructive and precipitates violence. For example, a parent can tell his child that it is right and proper to be angry because babies are being murdered through abortion by the millions. This is a righteous indignation. But it is wrong to have an uncontrolled anger that would cause a person to bomb an abortion clinic or murder an abortion doctor. Tell them that the proper physical response to the abortion issue is to "grow-up" and vote for congressmen and senators who are pro-life in philosophy.

Another way to manage anger in a child is to train him to express it through controlled verbal conversation. If a parent does not allow his child to verbally express his anger, it will only cause the child to suppress it, causing deeper emotional damage at a later time. When it does surface again, it will be in the form of depression, uncontrolled shouting, or physical violence.

Controlled verbal conversation is an appropriate "vent" for anger. A parent must be willing to allow his child to come to him and express his anger verbally. Unfortunately, a pit that many parents fall into at this point is to become angry themselves. When a parent responds to the anger of a child with anger, it forces the child to withdraw and push his anger inward. The parent usually interprets this as submission on the part of the child and thinks the problem is resolved. In reality, the child is responding to the parent's anger with fear rather than submission. He is only pushing his anger deeper into himself. This causes resentment which will eventually express itself with rebellion in the child.

Some children control their household with their anger. Parents who have never learned the importance of managing their child's anger will relinquish control of the household to the whims of their angry, spoiled, uncontrollable child. All the child has to do is throw a tempertantrum and mom and dad begin to act like puppets on a string, giving in to every "want" and "urge" of the child. They hope by doing so the child's anger will be appeased. In reality, all this does is reinforce his uncontrolled anger by rewarding it. Parents who struggle with this problem often go as far as making the other siblings of the household give-in to the angry child's desires. This sends confusing signals to the rest of the children in the household. It is telling them that if they want to get rewarded, they will have to do wrong, just as the angry child was rewarded for doing wrong. The end-result is total confusion.

Anger management must be learned. It is a discipline that a parent develops in his child through time and experience. Some parents think that their child's anger will go away as he grows older. In reality, the opposite is true. Uncontrolled anger actually magnifies the older the child gets. Tragically, its effect also magnifies. An angry toddler may throw food or a spoon. To the parents or other adults, the action may even be interpreted as "cute."

Unfortunately, as the angry child grows physically, so do his negative actions. As an adolescent, he may throw a fist. As a teenager he may throw a knife, or even a bullet

It's a Heart Thing

Changing the behavior of a child will not necessarily change what is in his heart. I am reminded of the story of a child who was in a grocery store with her mom. She kept standing up in the shopping cart until her mother finally said, "Mary, if you stand up one more time, I will spank you when we get home." The little girl immediately sat down, puckered her lips, folded her arms, looked at her mother, and said, "I am sitting down on the outside, but I am standing on the inside." This little story emphasizes the fact that it is important to do more than just change the temporary behavior of a child; we also must work at changing what is in a child's heart. Many parents have the concept backwards. They work hard at changing their child's behavior thinking that the results will change the child's heart. They are later shocked to find out that this has not happened. If a parent were to spend most of his time working at changing his child's heart, he will discover that the child's behavior will change accordingly.

It is far easier to set rules for a child to follow than it is to develop inner principles and convictions in a child's heart for him to live by. Outward rules and guidelines will be followed by a child as long as the fear of reprisal overrules the temptation. For example, a child will not smoke a cigarette as long as his fear of a whipping overrules the peer pressure that is placed on him by his friends. However, the moment the peer pressure of his friends becomes greater than his fear of reprisal, he will break the rules and smoke the cigarette.

On the other hand, if inner heart felt convictions have been developed, they will become the guiding compass that navigates the child through every decision of life. Even peer pressure has a hard time breaking through genuine heart-felt convictions that can be developed in a child. This is the purest meaning of Proverbs 22:6 that says, "Train up a child in the way he should go: and when he is old, he will not depart from it." In other words, if a parent develops convictions in a child when he is young, then when he is mature and on his own, he will not betray his convictions.

I have often heard parents make the statements, "I taught my child better than that!" "What has happened to him?" "Why is he now doing the things that I taught him not to do?" These parents dictated rules and demanded that they be followed by their children, but they never did develop convictions and principles of life in their hearts.

Chapter 5
Building With Style

Being a Balanced Parent

Every person who enters the arena of parenthood eventually develops a "parenting style." What I mean by "parenting style" is the attitude, mannerism of correction, and behavior a parent has in rearing his children. Unfortunately, just as no baby is born a perfect child, in like manner, no child grows into a perfect parent.

A good parent will adjust his "parenting style" to become a better parent. It is amazing how much better a child will become when his parent upgrades his parenting skills. For example, an attitude adjustment on the part of the parent will, more often than not, lead to an attitude adjustment on the part of the child.

In his book, Winning the Parenting War, David Clarke, Ph.D. states that there are five deviant "parenting styles":

1. The Overprotective Parent.
2. The Permissive Parent.

3. The Authoritarian Parent.
4. The Perfectionist Parent.
5. The Uninvolved Parent. (I like to call this style, The Pathetic Parent)

I will go into each of these "parenting styles" in some detail. Most parents have at least two of these styles of parenting going in their life at one time.

The Overprotective Parent

This "parenting style" produces a child that is safe, but stifled. A parent that adheres to this style of parenting does everything for his child. He picks up his dirty clothes, wakes him up in the morning, picks up his dirty dishes, caters every meal to his liking, and worse of all; fights his child's battles for him and bails him out when he gets into trouble. Pity the pastor, youth pastor, Sunday school teacher, secular school teacher, principal, or anyone else in authority who tries to call this child to accountability.

An overprotective parent tries to rear children in a low risk environment. A parent who uses this style tries to keep his child close at hand and attempts to limit his activities and associations to mostly within the home. If he lets his child out of his sight, he is certain that he will get involved playing ball or some other game with other kids; and you know how dangerous that is. Speaking of other kids, God forbid if his darling, little fragile child were to be mistreated by another child. If this happens, he will certainly race to his rescue, taking on the kid, his mom and dad, or anyone else involved.

The message an overprotective parent sends to his

child is that he can not make it on his own. Instead of developing independence, this style of parenting encourages dependence. This, in turn, destroys a child's confidence, creativity, and self-esteem.

Prior to my call into the ministry, I had earned a Bachelor and Post Graduate degree in the field of Botany. One of the things I learned studying the field of Botany is that a plant raised in a greenhouse environment is extremely hard to acclimate to its natural environment. The greenhouse environment is a highly controlled environment. Whereas a natural environment has fluctuating temperatures, unpredictable rainfall, harsh winds, plus other varying environmental factors. This is analogous to a child that is reared by an overprotective parent. This child never discovers what the real world is all about until it is too late to prevent it from having devastating effects on his life.

A parent must learn early on that he will not be able to shelter his child forever. This is unrealistic and unnatural. Sooner or later, in one way or another, the parent will cease to be in the picture and the child will meet the real world.

Let me add a little note of caution to the parents who are either "home schooling" their children or sending them to a Christian academy. Make certain that you are also developing the social side of your children's lives. You must gradually expose them to the "real world" that is out there, or just as the greenhouse plant, they will not survive if thrown into it unprepared. I encourage you to acclimate them to the real world while they are still in your home. By doing this, you can give them the support, encouragement, monitoring, and especially the guidance they will need while going through the process.

A parent must be willing to let his child experience

failure and pain (within reason). After all, this is a part of maturing and entering the world of adults. In other words, it is a natural part of "growing up."

The Permissive Parent

This "parenting style" follows the order of "submission in reverse." This is the type of parent who is always giving in to his child's demands. This parent is most often highly phlegmatic in personality. It is easy to understand why some parents succumb to this "parenting style." After all, it takes far less energy to give into a child's whims and demands than it does to put forth the effort to take a stand for that which is appropriate and right for the child. Many times, the parent who exercises this "parenting style" fears, that he will lose his child's love if he doesn't give in to his child's demands.

The child who is reared under this "parenting style" learns early on that mom or dad can't stand confrontation and will quickly "cave in" to any type of tantrum. If Johnny screams during church service, mommy will take him into the foyer and let him bounce from couch to couch and play until his devious little heart is content.
Children are born with an undisciplined, selfish, willful nature. An infant thinks that his only purpose in life is for people to cater to him and to satisfy his every desire. Corrie brought this reality home to Beverly and me when she was only a few months old. When Corrie was ready for her bottle (this was just prior to the "breast feeding era"), she would whimper in certain way for a few short seconds. We learned quickly that this was just a "warning shot" fired across the deck of our pleasant, peaceful, little home.

This was actually a two to three minute window of opportunity to get a bottle in the microwave, heat the formula to perfection, and get it inserted into Corrie's mouth. If we didn't make it in time, Corrie would proceed to punish us by refusing to take the bottle for about ten minutes. All the while, she would be screaming at the top of her lungs. For about six months, it became an interesting ritual in the Pavlu home. Corrie would whimper, and the "air raid drill" would begin. Beverly would fly to the refrigerator. I would be setting the microwave time, and we would both be praying that we would make it within Corrie's "two minute warning" time. John Elway had nothing on us. Most of the time we made it, but when we didn't, the punishment would begin. This continued over and over, until one day I took a stand. As usual, Corrie gave her little whimper signifying to us that she wanted her bottle immediately. However, this time we took our time getting it. When the "grace period" that Corrie had set was up, she began her tantrum. Only this time, when she had finished her tantrum, she still didn't get her bottle (the Child Protection Agency would really have a hay-day with this). After a few rounds of temper tantrums which yielded no bottle, Corrie came to the conclusion that the only way she was going to get a bottle was to whimper and then wait. This system worked well until she learned how to talk. Of course, that is another story.

    A mom or dad who exercises the "permissive style" of parenting usually sets few rules and guidelines, and rarely metes out any form of punishment when they are broken. The sad tragedy about this is that every time a rule is broken, and the child goes unpunished, he loses more respect for his parents and other authority figures in his life. A parent who does this is essentially telling his child that he does not have to respect others, and that he is not going to be held accountable for his actions. When this child reaches his teenage years, be becomes uncontrollable in every facet of his life. His mom and dad come to the shocking reality that because they never took control, they have now, by default, relinquished all control of their child's life. At this point, the "permissive parents" feel as if they are on a roller coaster going wherever the ride takes them.

A child who has been reared by "permissive parents" acquires the attitude that nothing is his fault. After all, mom or dad has always been there to clean up his messes upon demand. The end-result of this was that he was never given the opportunity to learn from his mistakes. Dr. David Clarke made this statement about a child reared by "permissive parents": (Page 35)

> *"She got that poor grade because the teacher was incompetent or didn't like her. She got that speeding ticket because that policeman had it in for her. She did pot because her friends pressured her. She skipped church because those other girls in the youth group were jealous of her and treated her badly. You are raising a liar, a manipulator, and a person who is unwilling to change and grow".*

The sad tragedy about "permissive parents" is that their motive is to make their child love them, but the end result is that their child loses all respect for them. The child later grows to hate them for it.

A child must have boundaries set in his life. It is a parent's responsibility to set the boundaries and to discipline his child when the boundaries are broken. A child will respect his parents for doing this and will later love and appreciate them for having put forth the effort to confront him, rather than having skirted the issues.

The Authoritarian Parent

This is the "parenting style" that produces "drill sergeant" dads and moms. This parent is usually choleric in personality. The parent who uses this style feels the deep need to be in control. He feels that he must be in control of every decision his child has to make. The child is not allowed to express his own ideas on any matter, and, may the Lord help him if he were to build enough courage to disagree with "sergeant dad." This would immediately be interpreted as rebellion or insubordination and be considered a personal attack on the parent's authority. The authoritarian parent will then retaliate by squelching the conceived insurrection by belittling or shaming the child until he is totally under his thumb again. The sad thing about this parenting style is that this type of parent truly feels that he is helping his child. In his mind, he feels that his child is incapable or unqualified to make decisions on his own.

One of the characteristics of an "authoritarian parent" can be found in the correction he metes out to his child. It is often overly harsh and administered for large and small mistakes, even minor infractions. The resulting effect on the child is that instead of respecting his parent, he fears him.

There are two important passages of scripture that apply to an "authoritarian parent":

And, ye fathers, provoke not your children to wrath: but bring them up in the nurture and admo-

nition of the Lord.

(Ephesians 6:4)

Fathers, provoke not your children to anger, lest they be discouraged.

(Colossians 3:21)

Ephesians 6:4 says that a father is not to provoke his child to wrath. Colossians 3:21 says that a father is not to provoke his child to anger. Wrath and anger are two key emotions that are manifested in young people who turn violent. A child who is constantly under the thumb of an authoritarian parent is never allowed to develop a relationship with him. Perhaps this is the greatest damage that is caused by this style of parenting. As the child grows older, he becomes embittered and angry with his parents, others, and life in general.

At some point the child who lives in the military environment that is produced by a drill sergeant parent is going to get fed up with the whole situation and go a.w.o.l. The only child who might make it through this parenting style is one that has a phlegmatic, passive, submissive, personality. However, these children will not make it into adulthood unscathed. They were never taught to think out problems for themselves. This weakness will show itself when they have families of their own. They were so trodden under foot and beaten down in childhood that they will not be able to take a stand for anything as adults.

If as a parent, you sense that you are being too authoritarian, back away from your desire to control your child by easing up on your harshness and hardness in the way that you are dealing with him. Above all else, learn how to develop a relationship with your child. Encourage him to give his opinion about various situations and issues, and don't jump down his throat when his opinion is contrary to your own. Allow him to make decisions on his own while you gently give him guidance in the background. Encourage him to express himself and don't cut him off, even when you don't agree with what he is saying. You will always have the chance later to correct his erroneous views. In other words, take off the drill sergeant uniform.

The Perfectionist Parent

This parenting style demands perfection out of imperfect children. Most of the time, this style of parenting is found in a parent with a melancholy personality. A perfectionist parent does not allow children to be children. He has zero tolerance for mistakes. He will demand that his child act as an adult while forgetting that even adults make mistakes. He resents the fact that his child disrupts his perfectly ordered world.

A child who is reared by a perfectionist parent feels that he can do nothing right. His little life is filled with stress and frustration. Every move that he makes is being observed, diagnosed, and continually corrected. Every miss-step in his life is quickly pointed out to him.

The attitude of a perfectionist parent is that it is his responsibility to inspect, analyze, and point out every mistake that his child makes. He only gives approval to his child when a task is done to an extremely high, almost unattainable standard of perfection. The parent then uses the excuse that he is trying to get his child to perform with excellence, not realizing that there is a great difference between unfeasible perfection and excellence. The end result is that he strips his child of all motivation to do anything right in life, because even after he does it, he still does not obtain his parent's approval.

The attitude of a child who is living under the bondage of a perfectionist parent is that anything he does is not going to be good enough, so why do anything! This parenting style focuses on the negatives of a child's life, rather than on his positive traits. This robs a child of his self-esteem. To get any approval from his parent, the child must perform to his parent's extreme and unreasonably high expectations. For example, 99% on an exam is not good enough because it could have been 100%; the lawn is never mowed right; the house is never cleaned right; the car is never washed right; the clothes are never folded right. The end result is frustration and anger with his parent and life in general.

A parent should challenge his child to reach for excellence, but at the same time set standards of achievement at a reasonable and achievable level. Learn to give praise to a child, not just at the completion of a job well done, but throughout the process. When he makes a few mistakes along the journey, help him to navigate back to the right path. At the same time praise him for each step that he takes in the right direction. This form of encouragement motivates a child to reach for excellence, while building on the relationship between the parent and the child at the same time.

The Uninvolved Parent

Another name for this parenting style would be the "pathetic parent." A person with this style of parenting prioritizes everything over his children. To the uninvolved parent everything is more important than his children. This may be a subconscious reality. Nevertheless, it is still a reality to the child. This parent's job, friends, hobbies, money, career, even household tasks, are more important than his children.

A parent who uses this style of parenting does not see the big picture. He has tunnel vision and can only see what makes him personally happy for the moment. He does this at the expense of disregarding the immediate needs of his children. He fails to see the Biblical, God-ordained descending order of priorities and that is God first, and immediately after God is his family. At the risk of sounding redundant, let me emphasize this! After God comes the Family. Next to God, nothing is above the family. This may come as a shock to some, but the family is even above the Church--for without families, there would be no Church. Within the family, priority is in this order: First is a person's responsibility to spouse; next is responsibility to children. As a husband and a father, my first responsibility is to my wife, immediately followed by my responsibility to my children.

As pathetic as it may sound, the bottom line in the uninvolved parent's world is meeting the personal wants in his life. Whatever he or she desires always comes first. Time and energy goes into whatever makes the parent happy without any regard for the happiness and well being of the children. The children only get the remnants of the parent's time.

When the uninvolved parent finally gets around to doing something with the children, it is done half-heartedly and without getting involved with them. The parent's mind is always somewhere else. He may be home with them, but he really has no meaningful conversation with them. Most communication is something like: "Go to your room" or "Go play outside." The parent rarely meets their child's friends or tries to get to know them. An uninvolved father doesn't have time to go outside and throw the ball with his children. After all, he has "important" things to do such as, watch the news, talk on the phone, read the newspaper, or work on the computer.

As sad as it may sound, the child of an "uninvolved parent" is constantly hungering for parental attention. He looks for him at special events at school or other special occasions, such as birthday parties or church presentations. However, this parent is just too busy to be there. In reality, the uninvolved parent is too busy meeting his own needs and does not realize that his selfishness is hurting his child. Year after year, the same scenario continues. The opportunity to build a relationship with and instill principles and virtues in his child is wasted. What a terrible price the parent and the child will pay in the future.

Have you ever seen a kid walking around with a chip on his shoulder? He resents most people with whom he comes into contact, and he resents life in general. Almost every child such as this can be traced back to an uninvolved parent. You can almost hear their cries: "Dad, where were you when I needed your instruction and guidance?" or Mom, where were you when I needed your nurturing and compassion?" When these young people reach adulthood and leave home, they may come back home and visit their parents on occasion, but there will always be awkwardness in their visit. Others will not come home at all, even during holidays. They will choose to act as if their mom and dad do not exist; after all, they are no more than strangers to each other anyway! Some will go through the motions of bringing the grandchildren around at Christmas or Thanksgiving, but there will be no true closeness or productive communication between them because there never was a relationship developed between them.

An uninvolved parent is much the same as a part-time Christian. A part-time Christian goes to church once or twice a month and, of course, every Easter Sunday unless something more important comes up. He gives "token offerings" and sometimes to a special fundraiser as long as it is not more than once every two or three years. Why, he even went to a special service last year when that "well known evangelist" was speaking. Most of the time he thinks that he actually is a pretty good Christian. The part-time parent also thinks he is doing pretty good in rearing his children until one day, he discovers that he is a stranger to the nearest and dearest thing to his heart--his own children.

The insensitivity of an uninvolved parent results in making his children feel that they are unimportant. Day after day, they see everything and everyone prioritized above them. This in turn destroys their self-esteem, which is then replaced by insecurity, anxiety, and loneliness. As a parent, you must get involved with your children. You have heard the old "quality time" or "quantity time" argument. I say, give them both! You don't have time to not give them time. I know that is a play on words, but whether you have noticed it or not, your children are rapidly growing into adults, with or without you.

The Balanced Parent

After having written so much about deviant parenting styles, I feel it would be appropriate to write a small summary on the style that every parent should develop in his quest for proper parenting. The reason this is only a summary is because the intent of this entire book is to develop balanced parents.

The "balanced parent" style is the God ordained style of parenting. It is a balance between unconditional love and unwavering boundaries. The "balanced parent" loves his child with unconditional, unselfish, steadfast love, and at the same time builds Godly, resolute, and firm boundaries around his child. Most importantly, this style of parenting tells a child that he is loved by his parents. It also builds self-esteem, creating a relationship between the parent and his child, while developing solid, secure boundaries that require a child to be accountable for his actions.

This parenting style does not just happen. On numerous occasions I have heard other parents say to me or Beverly statements such as, "You are lucky to have such well behaved, balanced children that truly love the Lord," or "I wish that God had given me good kids like He gave you." These parents actually think that it was just mere chance that Corrie, Jared, and Layna turned out the way that they did. They fail to see the hours on top of hours that were put into building up our children. To become a balanced parent, every one of us must reach beyond the weaknesses of our personality make-up and put forth the time, energy, commitment, and prayer to develop this style of parenting.

Chapter 6
Building Up Your Child

Planning for Your Child's Future

It is critical that a parent anticipates his child's needs, both physically and spiritually. Most parents have enough foresight to plan ahead for their child's education. They save in advance for the high cost of college. What about the emotional and Spiritual needs that he will have in the future? Have we planned for and anticipated this? Let me give you the Biblical example of two kings who are recorded in the Word of God.

The first is David. He planned ahead for Solomon his son to take the Kingdom and prosper in the work of God. Solomon is well known for two things. First, he built the beautiful temple of God. Next he is known as the wisest man of the Old Testament. However, what many people don't know is that David planned ahead for both of these things to happen in Solomon's future before Solomon was even King. This event is recorded in:

> *Then David said, This is the house of the LORD God, and this is the altar of the burnt offering for Is-*

rael. And David commanded to gather together the strangers that were in the land of Israel; and he set masons to hew wrought stones to build the house of God. And David prepared iron in abundance for the nails for the doors of the gates, and for the joinings; and brass in abundance without weight; Also cedar trees in abundance: for the Zidonians and they of Tyre brought much cedar wood to David. And David said, Solomon my son is young and tender, and the house that is to be builded for the LORD must be exceeding magnifical, of fame and of glory throughout all countries: I will therefore now make preparation for it. So David prepared abundantly before his death. Then he called for Solomon his son, and charged him to build an house for the LORD God of Israel. And David said to Solomon, My son, as for me, it was in my mind to build an house unto the name of the LORD my God: But the word of the LORD came to me, saying, Thou hast shed blood abundantly, and hast made great wars: thou shalt not build an house unto my name, because thou hast shed much blood upon the earth in my sight. Behold, a son shall be born to thee, who shall be a man of rest; and I will give him rest from all his enemies round about: for his name shall be Solomon, and I will give peace and quietness unto Israel in his days. He shall build an house for my name; and he shall be my son, and I will be his father; and I will establish the throne of his kingdom over Israel for ever. Now, my son, the LORD be with thee; and prosper thou, and build the house of the LORD thy God, as he hath said of thee. Only the LORD give thee wisdom and understanding, and give thee charge concerning Israel, that thou mayest keep the law of the LORD thy God.

(1 Chronicles 22:1-12)

David, first made preparation for the temple by gathering all of the materials needed to construct it. He then charged Solomon to build it. After David was through giving Solomon instructions on building the Temple, he next prayed that the Lord would give him wisdom and understanding concerning his dealings with the nation of Israel. This is found recorded in verse twelve. Notice how this comes to fruition in Solomon's life:

> *In that night did God appear unto Solomon, and said unto him, Ask what I shall give thee. And Solomon said unto God, Thou hast shewed great mercy unto David my father, and hast made me to reign in his stead. Now, O LORD God, let thy promise unto David my father be established: for thou hast made me king over a people like the dust of the earth in multitude. Give me now wisdom and knowledge, that I may go out and come in before this people: for who can judge this thy people, that is so great? And God said to Solomon, Because this was in thine heart, and thou hast not asked riches, wealth, or honour, nor the life of thine enemies, neither yet hast asked long life; but hast asked wisdom and knowledge for thyself, that thou mayest judge my people, over whom I have made thee king: Wisdom and knowledge is granted unto thee; and I will give thee riches, and wealth, and honour, such as none of the kings have had that have been before thee, neither shall there any after thee have the like.*
>
> *(2 Chronicles 1:7-12)*

Neither of these two things happened by chance in Solomon's life. David made preparations for his son's future. Always remember that, at least to some degree, a child's future is in his parent's hand.

The next king that I would like to bring to your attention is King Hezekiah. He was a good king who respected and obeyed the Word of God. This good king had one major short-coming. He only thought of himself and his personal comforts. He failed in the area of preparing for his children's future. This is vividly recorded in:

> *Then said Isaiah to Hezekiah, Hear the word of the LORD of hosts: Behold, the days come, that all that is in thine house, and that which thy fathers have laid up in store until this day, shall be carried to Babylon: nothing shall be left, saith the LORD. And of thy sons that shall issue from thee, which thou shalt beget, shall they take away; and they shall be eunuchs in the palace of the king of Babylon. Then said Hezekiah to Isaiah, Good is the word of the LORD which thou hast spoken. He said moreover, For there shall be peace and truth in my days.*
>
> *(Isaiah 39:5-8)*

Hezekiah made no attempt to intercede for his children whatsoever. He selfishly thought only of himself, that there would be peace and truth in his days.

Let me extend to you a word of caution. We must separate our personal dreams from what is important for our children's future. Many parents make the mistake of trying to relive their lives through their children. This is unfair to the children because God uniquely makes every child with his own personality mixture, giftedness, talents, desires, and aspirations. Therefore, we must give our children latitude to create, develop, and pursue their own dreams.

The Power of Parenting

A parent has the potential of being the strongest influence on a child's life. By taking both quantity and quality time to continually train up his child, a parent can supersede the influence that schools, peers, and Hollywood have on the child.

A parent may be thinking, "How can I compete with the school system that has my child six to seven hours a day, nine months out of the year?" In reality, a child is in school 180 days out of the year which totals to six months. The reason the total would seem to be nine months is that the 180 school days are stretched over a period of nine months. The other six months is an open calendar that a wise parent will use to instruct his child. Also, keep in mind that of the 180 school days, only six to seven hours of those days are spent in school. The other 17 to 18 hours per day are available for the parent to use in the training of his child. When observed from this perspective, the superior power that a public school has above the parent in influencing the child is a myth. If the parent will use the time and energy available to him wisely, he will have the advantage in developing the child.

Parents — The Ultimate Teachers

What a parent teaches his child about life has more influence on that child's perception than anything a teacher could teach in a classroom setting. When a parent builds a relationship with his child, he has a "secret weapon" that can not be transcended by anyone. That weapon is the "power of influence." A parent can influence his child to have the proper perception of life. Perception plays an essential role in the actions and lifestyle of a person. How a person perceives things determines the choices and decisions that he will make in life. If a child has a negative perception about life, family, church, or living for God, he will probably struggle with these areas as he matures. The old saying is true that "perception is everything." Let me give you an example from the Word of God:

> *And it came to pass after this, that the king of the children of Ammon died, and Hanun his son reigned in his stead. Then said David, I will shew kindness unto Hanun the son of Nahash, as his father shewed kindness unto me. And David sent to comfort him by the hand of his servants for his father. And David's servants came into the land of the children of Ammon. And the princes of the children of Ammon said unto Hanun their lord, Thinkest thou that David doth honour thy father, that he hath sent comforters unto thee? hath not David rather sent his servants unto thee, to search the city, and to spy it out, and to overthrow it? Wherefore Hanun took David's servants, and shaved off the one half of their beards, and cut off their garments in the middle, even to their buttocks, and sent them away.*
> *(2 Samuel 10:1-4)*

King Nahash, the king of the children of Ammon, although he was an enemy to the Children of Israel, had showed David kindness. When King Nahash passed away, David desired to return the kindness that King Nahash had shown him to his son, Hanun, by consoling him after the death of his father. The princes of Ammon insinuated that the ambassadors that David sent were under pretense of being comforters and were actually spies. Hanun's perception of David immediately changed. He took the ambassadors of David and did things to humiliate them, then sent them back to David. That which was meant for good by David was perceived as evil by King Hanun.

It is a parent's responsibility to give his child the proper perception of life. Teaching the basic elements of education, reading, writing, and arithmetic are the classroom teacher's primary responsibilities. At the same time, teaching a child how to build character, virtue, appropriate attitudes, and Godly principles are the parent's primary responsibilities.

Educators certainly have their role in teaching children, but they cannot do it all, nor should a parent get the attitude that they should do it all. Even those parents who send their children to a Christian academy should never get the attitude that the teachers of the academy have assumed the parent's role and responsibility of instilling principles and virtues in their children.

Some parents have the attitude that school is the "foundation of learning" for their child, and their only responsibility is to add bits and pieces of knowledge at home to the great reservoir of truth that has been placed into the child from the school environment. In reality, it should be the other way around. The home should provide the "ground of learning" for the child. To this foundation and structure of truth built by the parents, the teacher at school should add all other specialized information. The educator and the school system should only supplement what the child is being taught in the home. In other words, the parent should be the primary teacher of the principles of life from the child's birth to maturity. Notice that this concept was followed in the Old Testament Jewish culture:

> *Hear, O Israel: The LORD our God is one LORD: And thou shalt love the LORD thy God with all thine heart, and with all thy soul, and with all thy might. And these words, which I command thee this day, shall be in thine heart: And thou shalt teach them diligently unto thy children, and shalt talk of them when thou sittest in thine house, and when thou walkest by the way, and when thou liest down, and when thou risest up. And thou shalt bind them for a sign upon thine hand, and they shall be as frontlets between thine eyes. And thou shalt write them upon the posts of thy house, and on thy gates.*
>
> *(Deuteronomy 6:4-9)*

This is the classic scripture that portrays the role of a Jewish parent teaching his child the value system that he is to follow in life. The Jewish parent did not depend upon an educator or upon his Rabbi to teach his child. He looked upon himself as the primary instructor of his child. With diligence, he personally taught him in the home.

The Two Methods of Parenting

Most parents use the same methods and techniques to rear their children that their parents used upon them when they were growing up. This can be a good situation if their parents were skilled in the ways and manners of child rearing, which is often not the case. The examples that our parents set are often the model we choose in the rearing of our own children. Many parents fail to take the time and energy to examine the model they are using to see if it is the right model, or if it can be improved or refined.

According to Ross Campbell, M.D., there are two approaches to parenting. The first is reactive parenting, which responds primarily to what children do. The second is proactive parenting, which deals with and dispenses to children what they primarily need. Dr. Campbell says the following:

> *"The reactive approach results in punishment-oriented parenting. The proactive approach anticipates and then seeks to meet the most basic needs of children. This positive, proactive approach is the more effective way to rear children."*
>
> (Relational Parenting, Ross Campbell, M.D., p 12)

The problem with reactive parenting is that the parent is always one step behind the child. Instead of building a relationship with the child, the parent is spending most of his time in "crisis management." However, with proactive parenting, the parent is out front anticipating the child's needs and constantly providing an environment of safety, creativity, positive motivation, assurance, instruction, and love.

There are two verses of scripture that every parent should add to his repertoire of memorized verses. They are as follows:

> *And, ye fathers, provoke not your children to wrath: but bring them up in the nurture and admonition of the Lord.*
>
> *(Ephesians 6:4)*

> *Fathers, provoke not your children to anger, lest they be discouraged.*
>
> *(Colossians 3:21)*

A parent should evaluate himself in the light of these two scriptures to ensure that he is not causing some of the behavioral improprieties of his child. All parents will make mistakes. Mature parents will see their faults and do something about it.

Many times a parent's attitude and response to situations involving his children can become provocative. I find it amazing how the weaknesses of a person's personality always displays itself with the people he loves the most; notably his children and spouse. Actions and statements that a person would never display or say around people that are strangers to him will flow out like water coming from a broken dam onto his loved ones.

Often, a parent can be so calm, cool, and collected around others, yet be so out of control around his family. Perhaps, these people have the attitude, "To maintain my image, I have to be good around others, but I can just be myself around my family." This realization came to me one day when I was counseling (actually attempting to counsel) an irate teenager. I was very patient and composed with him. I calmly allowed him to vent his feelings and to spew out his feelings of anger and hatred toward his parents. At first, I was very proud of myself and my controlled temperament, and then, in afterthought, I began to feel guilty. If this would have been my son or daughter, would I have been as patient? Would I have given my child the opportunity to use me as a sounding board, or as someone to vent his feelings on? More than likely, in the midst of his venting, there would have been a nuclear explosion. The bomb would not have been dropped by him, but by me.

I know that this is a different twist on the scriptures about a parent not provoking his children to anger, but we must realize that it is often a parent's insensitivity or impatience that creates anger and rage within a child. Many times, a child's lack of communication with his parents, or one of his parents, is rooted in the reactive nature and attitude of the parent or parents. If a parent continuously goes into orbit every time his child has a minor mess-up in his life, it won't be long before the child learns to keep his mouth shut while his parent is on a rampage. The progression of this scenario then begins to expand into other areas, ultimately causing communication between the child and the parent to erode. The child eventually keeps his mouth shut, even when good things are happening. From this point on, there is a total breakdown in communication. However, remember that it did not start with the child, but with the reactive parent.

It is very important that a parent listen to his child, even if a negative situation is involved or a mistake has been made. It is also good to listen to a child when he is offering constructive criticism, if it is offered with the right spirit and attitude. After all, no one knows a parent better than his child and spouse.

If you have been a "reactive" parent, you may have to close in the gaps that have been created between you and your child by your negative actions. It is vital that you re-connect with your child if he is no longer communicating with you. The best way to begin is by being open with him. Admit to him that you have been reactive in dealing with him. Put this into his language. Say something like, "I know that I have been blowing my top a lot lately, but I am going to try and do better." If at this point, he spits out a little negative "venom," don't try to defend

> It is very important that a parent listen to his child, even if a negative situation is involved or a mistake has been made.

yourself. Let him know that you will seriously think about the information that he has just shared with you.

Many times it is not the facts, but a child's perception of the facts, that must be brought out and dealt with. As communication between a parent and his child is bridged, many of the misconceptions of the child will be clarified and brought into proper perspective.

This does not mean that there will not be times when a parent will have to deal "reactively" with his child. Those times will come and the Bible instructs a parent to deal "reactively" in such situations:

Foolishness is bound in the heart of a child; but the rod of correction shall drive it far from him.
(Proverbs 22:15)

He that spareth his rod hateth his son: but he that loveth him chasteneth him betimes.
(Proverbs 13:24)

The rod and reproof give wisdom: but a child left to himself bringeth his mother to shame.
(Proverbs 29:15)

As a child gets older and begins to mature, the process of child rearing should become more and more proactive. It should get to the point that in the child's later teens, if all has gone well, the process should be predominately proactive.

A parent must face the reality that the time will come in his child's life when he will become too old to spank. After the child has moved out of the home, or married, he will become too old to correct. This does not mean that he will be too old to instruct. If he asks for instructions, or desires suggestions from his parents, give them. Hopefully there will be a smooth transition from a child to a mature independent adult, if the parent has operated under a proactive philosophy of child rearing from the child's birth.

The Domineering Parent

All children are born with a unique personality make-up. If they are allowed to, they will naturally flow into the characteristics of the blend they were born with. A domineering parent will not allow his child to find his own identity. This type of parent tries to make his child act just like he acts. The domineering parent never allows his child to develop his own personality and does not understand when his child responds to circumstances differently than the way he does. This greatly limits what the child can do, stifling his potential. A young child will submit to this type of control, but as he grows older, he will become angry, resentful, and rebellious.

The problem magnifies itself if the domineering parent is the mother and is accompanied by a weak father. Dr. Paul D. Meier in his book, Christian Child-Rearing and Personality Development, states that his research found that the majority of neurotic children whom he treated came from homes in which there were weak, passive fathers and domineering, smothering, overprotective mothers. He went on to say that research literature describes hundreds of syndromes, and in a majority of them, there was a weak, passive father, and a domineering, smothering, overprotective mother.

A domineering parent often makes the mistake of trying to possess his child. He controls every move the child makes. As the child grows older and should be in the process of learning to make decisions for himself, the possessive, domineering parent will continue to maintain strong control over his life and make every decision for him. The parent may do this while showing strong expressions of love to the child. For this reason, the child may not realize that he is being controlled by his parent.

A parent must remember that he does not own his child. He is a creation of God and has been placed under the trust of a parent who is given the sacred responsibility of "training him up in the way he should go."

Don't Put Them on a Guilt Trip

There are some children who have a personality make up which creates within the child a deep desire to please others. This occurs primarily in children who are extremely melancholy and to a lesser degree in children that are phlegmatic. When a child of this personality mixture feels that he has not pleased his parents or other authority figure, he feels guilty. This particular type of child is easily controlled. Herein lies the danger. Some parents, especially those of a choleric nature, take advantage of this guilt to control their child and make him act against his will to do what they want him to do. Rather than being trained-upward to think for himself and to become self-sufficient, he becomes subservient to a stronger personality. This weakness later shows itself when people of stronger personality suggest that he do something wrong, illegal, or immoral. For example, when a friend or neighbor suggests the use of drugs or other wrong doing, he will try to please them by doing it.

Don't have unreasonable expectations of a child. If a parent expects to mold his child into a faultless person with ideal character traits, he is setting himself up for a great disappointment. Some parents tend to forget that there are no perfect children in this world. At the same time, it is a parent's responsibility to encourage his child to reach for excellence in all that he does. A parent must realize the important role that he plays in molding his child's philosophies and character. Above all the influencers in a child's life, a parent has the greatest opportunity to make a positive difference in the character that a child will eventually chose to develop in his life.

A child's allegiance is usually to his parents until early or mid-adolescence. At this point, his allegiance tends to shift toward his peers. If a parent has done a good job with instilling character and virtues into his child, then the child will usually choose peers that have the same value system that his parents have taught him.

Training Up Your Child

Parenting is not just controlling the behavior of a child, but it is also giving guidance and instruction to him. This enables and equips him to reach his potential in life. Behavioral modification in a child is vitally important, but it should never be done at the expense of tearing down the child. Nowhere in the scripture is there any insinuation that a parent tearing down his child is condoned.

Training up means the opposite of tearing down. A parent must learn to rear his child with purpose. He must learn to stay in control of situations that come his way as a result of child rearing. There must be purpose in his actions toward his child. The scriptures say that a parent is to train his child upward:

Train up a child in the way he should go: and when he is old, he will not depart from it.
(Proverbs 22:6)

And, ye fathers, provoke not your children to wrath: but bring them up in the nurture and admonition of the Lord.
(Ephesians 6:4)

As long as a parent is in control of his household, he is training or building his children upward. When a child is in control of the household, there is chaos and confusion. All manner of harm comes form this and the end result is that the child is "trained down" instead of being "trained up."

There are two basic "truths" that are found in

Proverbs 22:6. The first is in the form of a promise. God is saying that you can be successful as a parent. You have the authority to rear children into productive Christian adults. This within itself should give all of us as parents a great hope. Even during the tough trying times that we will have in rearing our children through every stage of life from infants to adults, we can anchor or hope in this promise.

The next truth in this verse of scripture tells us that a child is not going to become a productive, wise, Godly, Christian adult by accident. As parents, we must put out the personal effort and sacrifice to "train up our child in the way he should go." We must have a game plan. We have to have a clearly defined course of action. Dr. Paul D. Meier, M.D. in his book Christian Child-Rearing and Personality Development states that approximately 85 percent of a person's adult personality is formed by the time he is six years old. He goes on to say that although it is not too late to correct a child's emotional defects after he has passed the age of six, it will become progressively more difficult. Statistically, the average child will live to about eighty years of age. This means that a child will carry the positive and negative traits of his personality that was developed in him during the first six years of his life, for the remaining seventy-four years of his life. This is a wake-up call to parents with young children. This emphasizes how crucial it is for a parent to train up a child, with emphasis on the word, "child", in the way he should go. Much of the potential for success or failure is programmed into a child in the crucial first six years. The sooner a parent plots out his course of action in training up his child, the better the results will be.

Nothing influences a child more than the training he receives at home from his parents. I am not down playing the importance of church, youth services, cell groups, and Sunday school. I know they too play an important role in touching the lives of children and young people. However, the greatest amount of time a child spends (at least, it should be this way), is with his parents. Compare this to the few hours that are allocated to a church setting. A parent must take the responsibility that has been placed into his hands seriously.

Train your child upward. Point out to him the ladder of success and give him instructions on how to climb it. Remember, your child was created in the "Image of God." If you will look at the potential of your child with this thought in mind, it will give you the motivation to inspire him to excel in life. God is not an "average god," He is The God of Excellence. I have always told my children that "C's" are not accepted in our household. In this hour of low standards anyone can make a "C." The definition of average in our modern day society is based on a very low scale. God expects His children to do all things with a "spirit of excellence." Inspire your child to always think of himself as a person with the potential of excellence. If he will think of himself in this manner, it will not only reflect itself on his report card, but it will manifest itself in every facet of his life; on the job, with relationships, with family, with friends, and eventually with perpetuating the same concept of "excellence" in his children. What an exciting thought! The "spirit of excellence" perpetuated from generation to generation in your own family.

Chapter 7
Building Character

It Takes a Parent

Hillary Clinton, the former "First Lady" of the United States said, "It takes a village to raise a child." Yet, the Bible says it takes a parent. The responsibility is not for a school, day care, church, or even a nation; but for a parent. All of the above can be tools that help in the process, but the ultimate responsibility is in the hands of the parents. The Bible admonishes parents:

> *Train up a child in the way he should go: and when he is old, he will not depart from it.*
> *(Proverbs 22:6)*

> *And, ye fathers, provoke not your children to wrath: but bring them up in the nurture and admonition of the Lord.*
> *(Ephesians 6:4)*

It is imperative that parents understand that there are many philosophies in our society that are diametrically opposed to the principles of the Word of God. Our children are exposed to these on a daily basis. The Bible says that we are in the world, but are not of the world. It is our responsibility to counter these destructive philosophies and instill virtues and principles in their place.

Building Respect for Others

In the 1940's and 1950's, parents required their children to respect adults. This included parents, teachers, principles, public leaders, Sunday school teachers, youth leaders, pastors, and other authority figures.

When a child was disciplined at school for any reason, he would receive another dose of discipline from his parents when he returned home. Parents tended to reinforce the efforts of the teacher and principal in the correction of their children. Likewise, the teacher and principal reinforced the efforts of the parents.

Today, the trend is in the opposite direction. If a teacher dares to discipline a student, he can expect to have an irate mother or father demanding a meeting with him and the principal the next day. The parent will believe the story of his immature, manipulative, devious, and irresponsible child above the words of a mature professional whose job is to try and instill an education into children in an orderly fashion. Usually the discussion between the parent and the teacher begins something like this, "Why are you always picking on my child?" The teacher responds, "What makes you feel this is happening"? The parent responds, "Because my child told me this is happening!" In other words, the parent always assumes that his child is right and always tells the truth and the teacher is always wrong, incompetent, uncaring, and really has something against his child. Now plug in another name for teacher such as Youth Pastor, Sunday school teacher, neighboring parent, police officer, and you get the point. No wonder the children of this generation have little or no respect for men and women in authority after they grow into adulthood.

As a parent, we must remember that it is in the nature of a child to want to blame others. It all started in the Garden of Eden. Adam sinned. Adam blamed Eve. Eve blamed the devil. The devil didn't have a leg to stand on. To reinforce this concept, let me ask you, have you ever heard a child that has just been in a heated argument with another child say unto him, "You are right and I am absolutely at fault". He would rather eat spinach or broccoli than admit that he is wrong.

After having reared three children, not one time have I mediated an argument between two of my children where I have heard one child spontaneously stop in the middle of the argument and say, "He's right, I'm wrong." Yet, common sense says that they can't both be totally right all of the time. Even armed with this knowledge, there are some over-protective parents or grandparents who will go to bat for their child with the biased philosophy that everything their sweet, darling, perfect, little angelic child (brat) is telling them about their mistreatment by the teacher or some other authority figure is true. Now I know that there can be times when the child is truly being mistreated. However, statistically this is the exception and not the rule.

Now you may ask the question, "What if I defend the person in authority over the story that my child is telling me, and later find out that my child was in the right?" I can remember this happening once with Jared, my middle child. Bear in mind, this was one incident out of hundreds of times that he was in the wrong. I forget the actual details of the incident. The part I do remember is giving Jared correction and later finding out that he was right. The first thing I did after verifying that he was right was to apologize to him. I then told him not to take it personally because it helped balance the scale for all the times he was wrong and I didn't find out about it. I let him know that he was still ahead of the game. We both walked away smiling.

Let me briefly speak on the other side of the coin. In the 1940's and 1950's, teachers used to uphold family values in the public school system. It is now tragic what is being taught in the schools of the third Millennium. Children are taught that the abomination of homosexuality is simply an "alternate lifestyle." They are taught that it is illegal to publicly pray during school hours or in a school-sponsored function. They are given condoms without parental consent and if the condoms do not work and they become pregnant, they can obtain an abortion without their parent's knowledge or consent. Society is in the throws of a negative paradigm shift and, we as parents must walk the tight rope of teaching our children respect for authority and taking a stand for that which is anti-Christian in the authority system of the 2000's.

Building a Positive Image of Others

As we rear our children, we are shaping their perception of people and the world around them. When I was a little boy, my mom, due to her background and up bringing, constantly told me not to trust anyone. She taught me that I should always remember that everyone had an ulterior motive or hidden agenda. She instilled in me that everyone was always out to get me. Consequently, it took me coming to the Lord and the power of the Holy Ghost in my life for me to overcome this flawed philosophy of life.

While rearing our children, Beverly and I were extremely cautious about saying anything negative about other people, especially people that were part of our local assembly. I have noticed that many children that were raised in a minister's home walk around with a chip on their shoulder. They have heard their parents constantly talk about the problematic saints in their church. By the time they become teenagers, their perception of the church is that it is just a bunch of mean, ornery, contentious, people that give Dad and Mom a lot of trouble. Unfortunately, Mom and Dad have instilled within them such a negative view of the church that when it comes time for them to seek after the Lord, the last place they would look for Him is in that church with all of those bad, corrupt, and evil church members.

This same concept applies not only to pastors, but also to church members. If you are a layperson in your church, and all you talk about is how bad the other church members are, or how bad the pastor is, or other leaders in the church such as the youth pastor, or the Sunday school teacher, you will effectively destroy the positive impression that your child should have of the members of his church. Do not be surprised when your child gets older and expresses to you that he does not want to attend your church.

When our first child was born, Beverly and I committed to each other that Corrie would never hear us say anything negative about anyone in the church. If there were a problematic church member (I am sure that you probably have never had any of those in your church) we would discuss the situation privately, always away from the children. We would only speak of the good qualities of these people in front of our children. We taught them that you can always find something good to say about any person if you look hard enough. We faithfully adhered to this principle in the rearing of all three of our children. The results of this were manifold. To this day our kids have a positive attitude toward the church and those in it.

What Are Your Children Being Exposed To?

Statistics tell us that the only thing that the average child logs in more hours doing than watching television is sleeping. Do not allow Hollywood to be the predominant investor in your child's value system.

I have never allowed a television in our home. Looking back, I can honestly say that this was one of the best things that ever happened to my family. While other children were being exposed to scene after scene of violence, murder, drug abuse, nudity, adultery, and anti-Biblical principles, my children were being exposed to good books, abundant family time, and the opportunity to use their mind to be creative. As a result of this, my children have a far more realistic view of what real life is all about, and not the flawed view of Hollywood.

Work On the Weaknesses

Every child has his own unique personality. Found within that personality is a mixture of both strengths and weaknesses. Just as important as playing to a child's strengths, a parent must also work on eliminating or at least helping a child learn to control his weaknesses. To do this a parent must first identify the key weaknesses that are in his child's personality mix. These can be such things as stubbornness, rebellion, anger, and deviousness, to mention a few. The Bible calls these "Sin that easily besets us." Parents must begin to work or those weaknesses while the child is very young.

Wherefore seeing we also are compassed about with so great a cloud of witnesses, let us lay aside every weight, and the sin which doth so easily beset us, and let us run with patience the race that is set before us.
(Hebrews 12:1)

A few years ago, Hurricane Lili struck the south Louisiana coast. The eye of the storm passed very close to our house. I have 20 acres of pine trees growing in my back yard. They are in various stages of growth from 4-year-old saplings to 18-year-old trees. After the stormed passed, I went outside and surveyed the damage. I had over a thousand trees either bent sideways or flat on the ground. I spent the next two months straightening trees. I first straightened the 4-year-old saplings. In less than a minute, I would hit two wooden stakes into the ground, tie a piece of twine to the top of the tree, and straighten it. In a short period of a few days, I had straightened over 800 of them. My next task was to work on the 18-year-old-trees. That was a totally different situation. There were close to 200 that were severely bent sideways. With a come-along and heavy rope, I began the project of straightening the trees. I would tie the rope about two thirds up the tree, and instead of using stakes, I would tie the rope to other nearby standing trees. I would then use the come-along and attempt to winch the tree straight again. I managed to straighten 2 of the 200. The rest had to be cut down with a chain saw and burned.

The same concept is true for children. While they are young, they can easily be straightened. As they grow older, it becomes harder to deal with their weaknesses and character flaws. Adults with character problems did not develop these problems after they became mature adults. Negative character patterns develop early in a child's life and then magnify during adulthood. No wonder Proverbs 22:6 says that we are to train up a child in the way he is to go and that when he is old he will not depart from it. The positive side of this verse is that if a child is trained up with character, when he is a mature adult, he will not depart from the character that was placed into him. On the other hand, if the child is allowed to retain his character flaws as he grows older, he will not depart from those flaws as an adult.

We must "parent" in the present with the realization that the decisions we make today will affect our children in the future. We must make decisions that will develop our children's character. If we build character in our children, it will allow them to navigate through life securely, joyfully, and productively. Every parent wants his child's future to go well. The greatest assurance of this happening is accomplished through the process of "building character." We must "parent" in the present with the realization that the decisions we make today will affect our children in the future.

One of the character flaws that most children manifest at a very young age is the desire to control those around them, especially their parents. They do this by using the parent's emotion of fear. Now this is a character flaw that is stronger in some children than others, depending on the child's personality mixture.

My oldest daughter, Corrie, tried this when she was a little over one year old. It was getting her bedtime so Beverly told her she would have to put her play toys away to prepare her for bed. Corrie proceeded to fall to the floor, kicking her legs as if she had just learned how to break dance. She then took a big breath and held it. Now I had heard of other children who had done this before, and I had already rehearsed in my mind what I would do in a similar situation. The only problem was that I had not thought to share this plan with Beverly. As would be expected, with fear in her heart, as any good mother would have under a similar situation, Beverly quickly reached down to pick Corrie up. I immediately stopped her and whispered in her ear that I wanted us to ignore Corrie. Looking back on this event over twenty plus years later, it is comical to remember the look of shock that was in Beverly's eyes at that moment. I am sure she thought her sweet darling little baby girl was going to hold her breath until she expired from this life, and that mean old Daddy was just going to sit back and let it happen. What actually happened was that Corrie finally got tired of holding her breath and decided that it was much more comfortable to resume breathing. At this point, I picked her up, told her in "baby language" that her behavior was a "no-no" (spanked her), and then brought her to her baby bed and told her it was time for "night-night." She immediately fell asleep and to this day has never thrown another temper tantrum. We had called her bluff, thus making her realize that even at her young age, she could not manipulate us with the emotion of fear.

Another incident occurred with my youngest daughter, Layna. Again, the emotion of fear was the attempted method of manipulation. Layna was approximately four and one half years old. It was getting approximately her bedtime, and Beverly told her that she needed to pick up her toys to prepare for bed. She responded by telling her mother that she was not through playing. At this point, I took over and told her to do what her mother had said. She looked at me and said that if I made her do it, she would "run away." I was momentarily caught off-guard. However, I recovered immediately, and asked her where she was going to "run away" to. She thought for a little while, and then said she would run away to the trailer (We had a 12 by 50 trailer that we had lived in for a number of years before building our house. It sat in our back yard approximately 100 feet away from the house's back door). I jumped up from the chair in which I had been sitting and said to her that I would help her in this venture of "running away." We packed up her toys that were on the floor. We then went to her bedroom and packed some clothes and put them in a bag. We next went to the kitchen, put some cookies in another bag, grabbed her bag of clothes and toys, and stepped outside. Now we live in the country, and it seemed that on this particular night, that the darkness outside was magnified. I even commented to Layna on how dark it was. By the time we got to the trailer, I noticed that Layna was walking so close to my side that she was brushing my leg. I next unlocked the door to the trailer. It had not been opened for a few weeks and the door squeaked on its hinges. I put the toys, her bags of clothes, and cookies on the floor and explained to her that it was too expensive to turn the electricity on in the trailer, but that I knew she would understand that such things occurred when little girls "ran away" from home. She took one look in that dark trailer, climbed up in my arms and said, "Daddy, I don't think I want to run away from home. I want to go to the house and go to bed." From that day until now, Layna has never again threatened to "run away."

Tragically, many parents never overcome the fear oriented manipulative power of their children. The parents end up being controlled by the children instead of the children being controlled, guided, and balanced by the parents. As the children grow into adulthood, this character flaw magnifies. It grows to the point that it affects, not only the parents, but friendships, relationships, and eventually their marriage.

Unfortunately, our society has, in some ways, encouraged children to manipulate their parents through the use of fear. From a young age, our children are taught by social workers and child protection agencies that they can threaten their parents with being "turned in" to the Child Protection Agency. Now I know that this agency plays an important and essential part in protecting children from genuine child abuse, neglect, molestation, and other terrible crimes against children. Unfortunately, for the wayward child, total manipulation is just a phone-call away.

Chapter 8
Building a Safe Environment

Children and a Positive Home Environment

Parents are human. They have mood swings. There are no "Super-Moms" or "Super-Dads" out there. At the same time, a parent must be aware of the fact that his mood swings do affect his children. When a parent is going through troubling times as a result of his marriage, job, finances, or other stressful situations, and as a result becomes depressed, unhappy, discouraged or fretful, the child can misinterpret these as rejection.

Young children receive communication from their parents emotionally long before they receive communication verbally. When a parent is in a stressful situation, the child may feel "cut-off" emotionally from the parent. It is the responsibility of the parent to do his best to maintain a positive environment at home.

When a child's home is secure, he will feel at peace. Home becomes a refuge from his stress-filled world. The twenty first century has become a complex time for children. For this reason, every child needs the safe haven of a secure home. If a parent is providing this kind of refuge for his child, he need not expect his child to thank him for it. More than likely the child will not even recognize it for what it is. But if it is not there, the child will certainly recognize its absence.

As a pastor, I have had to deal with emotionally dysfunctional parents on various occasions. These parents strive to have their emotional needs met through their children. When they discover that their children were not designed to meet their emotional needs, they feel let down. In the plan of God, children were never given the responsibility of meeting the needs of the parents. Rather, parents were given the command to meet the needs of their children. Emotionally dysfunctional parents wreak havoc on the emotional well-being of their children.

Dr. Paul Meier in his book Christian Child-Rearing and Personality Development tells of ten easy steps for developing a normal, healthy baby into a drug addict or alcoholic. They are as follows:

1. **Spoil him; give him everything he wants if you can afford it.**

2. **When he does wrong, you may nag him, but never spank him (unless he is showing signs of independence).**

3. **Foster his dependence on you, so drugs or alcohol can replace you when he is older.**

4. **Protect him from your husband and from all those mean teachers who threaten to spank him from**

time to time. Sue them if you wish.

5. Make all of his decisions for him, since you are a lot older and wiser than he is. He might make mistakes and learn from them if you don't.

6. Criticize his father openly, so your son can lose his own self-respect and confidence.

7. Always bail him out of trouble so he will like you. Besides, he might harm your reputation if he gets a police record. Never let him suffer the consequences of his own behavior.

8. Always step in and solve his problems for him, so he can depend on you and run to you when the going gets tough. Then when he is older and still hasn't learned how to solve his own problems, he can continue to run from them through heroin or alcohol.

9. Just to play it safe, be sure to dominate your husband and drive him to drink too, if you can.

10. Take lots of prescription drugs yourself, so that taking non-prescription drugs won't be a major step for him.

Dr. Meier next tells how to develop a normal child into a homosexual. This is what he states in his book:

1. Start out by using the ten easy steps followed by the alcoholic's mother, but this won't be enough.

2. Show your love for your son by protecting him very

carefully. Don't let him play football or baseball with the boys—he might get hurt! Don't let him be a newspaper boy or patrol boy; he might catch pneumonia out in the bad weather.

3. Be sure he spends lots of time with you and very little with his father (or any other adult males).

4. Teach him to sew and cook, and how to knit too. After all, sexist attitudes about chores are out of date nowadays.

5. Walk him to and from school so none of his bullies will beat little Johnny up.

6. Let him play consistently with the little neighborhood girls or his sisters and their friends. There just aren't any boys his age in the neighborhood that you would want him to play with.

7. Joke with him about the feminine name you gave him, and tell what a cute girl he would have been. Tell him that you really had wanted a girl and dressed him in his big sister's clothes when he was little. That way, when he reaches puberty and his contemporaries start falling in love with the opposite sex, he can too—with boys, since he thinks of himself basically as a girl.

All parents have to grow older. They have no choice in this matter. However, age and maturity are not synonymous terms, nor does age automatically produce maturity. Maturity is a series of choices that a parent must actively make.

Healthy Marriages — Healthy Children

The most important place for a child to be given a demonstration of love is in the home. A healthy home is an ideal environment for meeting the emotional needs of children. When a husband and wife work on building a good marriage relationship they are also investing in the creation of an atmosphere that conveys the message of love to their children. One of the most important things that a parent can do for his child is to love his spouse.

A parent, especially a mother who does not receive emotional fulfillment from her husband, tends to look for it in her children. This will move her in the direction of co-dependency with them. Signs of co-dependency will begin to manifest themselves. These will be in the form of over protectiveness and control. She will become so desperate for a relationship with her child that she will fear to correct him when he manifests inappropriate behavior. She will tend to spoil and smother him, while making every decision for him. Activities with other children his age will be perceived by her to be competition for his attention. Thus, those activities will be limited, if allowed at all.

This is the age of "broken homes" and "broken marriages," which usually result in "broken children." If there is continual strife between a child's mom and dad, it will cause the child to feel a deep sense of insecurity. One of the greatest fears that a child faces today is the break-up of his home. Statistically, over half of his friends and peers with whom he associates live in a broken home. As he goes to school and plays in the neighborhood with so many kids from broken homes, it is only natural that he will begin to wonder if his mom and dad will be the next to break-up. These feelings of insecurity and doubt are reinforced each time he sees and hears his parents in conflict and strife with one another.

Children who constantly hear their parents arguing and verbally attacking one another are nearly always insecure children. When there are major marital problems that are unresolved in a home, the child will often become confused as to what love really is. "Mommy and Daddy are supposed to love each other and are suppose to love me, but look how they are acting with each other." "Does that mean that is the way they also love me?" Marital conflict can convey mixed messages to the minds of children.

Wise parents will deal with problems and issues of marriage in a private manner and at such times when the child is isolated and insulated from the parents' problems. The greatest contribution that parents can make to their child's emotional well-being is to keep their marriage healthy and strong.

The Dad & Mom Team

When it comes to rearing children, you and your spouse are a team. You must show your children a "united front!" You must both be united in purpose and in plan. For some reason, probably because of the nature that they inherited through Adam, children are born "con-artists." In fact, they are the greatest con-artists in the world. If there is any disunity between a mom and a dad concerning methodology of child-rearing, family rules, or concepts of discipline, children will immediately recognize it and use it against their parents. If they can find any opportunity to play one parent against the other, they will do it every time without an ounce of guilt.

To have teamwork, you and your spouse must take the time to develop a game plan. This arrangement should include creating the rules of the household, the method of correction when the rules are broken, and total agreement to back one another in front of the children.

I cannot over emphasize the importance of backing one another up! Never go behind your spouse's back and side with your child. He will immediately see this as a weakness in you, and exploit it to the fullest. This will result in destroying your effort to create accountability in his life. If you are not in agreement with your spouse over some decision that he or she has made concerning the children, don't tell the children. Rather, tell your spouse privately, and never in front of the children. If a child can discern even the slightest difference between mom and dad concerning any situation, he will use it to his advantage. He doesn't learn to do this. As I said earlier, it's just in his nature and a parent must be prepared for this.

A united plan doesn't evolve overnight. It takes time and planning on a continual basis. Neither is a plan that was developed for a young child relevant to a teenager. After all, kids are always getting older and every maturity level in their life creates new circumstances that must be addressed. For example, telling little Johnny at age two that the rule of the house is not to play with the "whatnots" on the coffee table is a far cry from telling John that his curfew is 11:00 P.M. on Friday night when he is out on a date at age seventeen. Changing circumstances demand changing the "game plan."

For a mom and dad to communicate, agree, or compromise their decisions as to what will be the rules of the household, is never an easy matter. A mother and a father must ever keep in mind that they are two uniquely different genders. A mother will think and come to her conclusions more from the right side of her brain where the emotion center is. A father will think and come to his conclusions more from the left side of his brain where the logic center is. To compound the differences, the mother and father both have different blends of personality, and the basic rule of thumb is that opposite personalities attract. In other words, the reason you are probably married to the person who is your spouse is because he or she has the opposite personality of yours. On the most part, choleric personalities usually marry phlegmatic personalities, and sanguine personalities usually marry melancholy personalities. Last but not least, you both come from two totally different family backgrounds. Remember to factor all of this into the equation when you are both trying to come to the same conclusion in developing a master plan for rearing your children and the accompanying rules of the household that will make this happen.

  No matter how you disagree with your spouse, the bottom line in presenting a united front to your children is to work it out, iron it out, hash it out, compromise, do whatever it takes. However, when you both step in front of your children, be 100% in accord with your rulings to your children. This almost sounds like a court of law, doesn't it? I have always been of the opinion that lawyers are not developed in law school. They come from little kids who seem to have one purpose in mind, and that is to discover one shred of incongruence or disagreement between their parents in regards to family rules.

When Parents Become Nerds

When children reach early adolescence, it is not uncommon for them to become intensely private. Whereas, a few months earlier, a child may have been communicating non-stop with his parents about anything and everything, suddenly without any identifiable reason, it seems that a stranger has taken over his body. Usually at this stage in the child's life, his parents transform from being "cool people" into "nerds" or people from the prehistoric era. A parent should never take this personally. He has not really changed, only in his child's new philosophy of thinking has he changed (It's an adolescent thing).

In the child's mind, it would be impossible for his old, out of date, ancient parents to relate to him now that he is such a modern, intelligent, up-to-date, young person. At this same time, the child will also begin to demand more privacy and more independence. This leaves the parent with a serious dilemma. It is at this stage in the child's life that the parent must know where he is at all times, who he is associating with, and who he is talking to on the phone. At the same time, the parent must respect his child's need for a certain amount of privacy.

The need for privacy is usually the first motions in a child's natural progression from dependence to independence. During this period of time in his child's life, a parent feels as if he is tip-toeing through a minefield. It is essential during this phase of the child's life, that the parent keep the lines of communication open, even if he has to do ninety percent or more, of the talking. At the same time, listen carefully to the few statements that the child will reciprocate during the lopsided conversations. Draw as much information as is possible out of him; at the same time, the parent must assure the child that he understands and respects his need for privacy. A parent should not excessively pry into every little detail of his child's life during this period of time. At the same time, be firm about knowing the answers to the important questions concerning the child's life such as: Who is he associating with? Who is influencing him? What are the philosophies and beliefs of the young people with whom he is associating? Where is he going when he leaves the house? Who is he talking to on the phone?

Your Children & Their Friends

It is a parent's responsibility to carefully examine the children or young people with whom his child associates or develops a relationship. This is a major factor that will determine the direction a child will take in life. If a child wants to spend time with and share ideas with another child, the parent should take the time to learn what system of values, principles, and virtues the child has been raised under. A parent must never forget that other children's values and ideas will eventually influence the way his child will eventually think and act.

I have heard the old cliché that a parent can't choose his children's friends. While there may be some element of truth to this statement, for the most part, it is not totally true. Beverly and I always chose the other children that Corrie, Jared, and Layna associated with. We were not able to control who they associated with at school or at some church function such as at a youth service, but we were able to control who they spoke to on the phone, invited over to the house, visited at other homes, etc. In other words, their discretionary time was under our control. This created a natural channeling effect that moved them toward other children that were raised with the same standards, principles, and values as theirs.

A parent must create a balance between the time his child spends with his family and the time he spends with his friends. There are "two ditches" involved in this scenario. One ditch that some parents fall into is to require their children to spend all of their discretionary time with their family. The other ditch that parents fall into is to allow their children to spend all of their discretionary time with their friends. Both of these extremes are wrong, and can set up dangerous and destructive circumstances. Part of a child's quest for independence revolves around his desire to have close personal friends to spend time with. A child's desire for independence will often cause him to withdraw from his family. Unfortunately, the independence drive hits at the age when the child needs the most direction and guidance from his parents. The issue is resolved by balancing the time a child spends with friends with the time he spends with his family.

Kids & Freedom

A parent should express to his child, while he is still young, that he will be given freedom in direct proportion to his maturity level and the accompanying trust that he earns through proper behavior as he grows older. Explain to him that there will be limited freedom at first and that more freedom will be given to him as he demonstrates that he is prepared to handle that freedom. This does two positive things. First, it gives a child something to look forward to. The child knows that the day will eventually come when he will attain his freedom. Next, it puts the parent in the "driver's seat." In other words, the parent, not the child, will make the determination as to when his child is to be given more freedom.

Remember, it is normal for children to push the rules of the household to their limits. A parent must be prepared for this. Children have a keen ability to become quite dramatic when they are trying to have their own way. A parent will often feel like a heel when his child is through presenting his highly thought out argument about how the rules he is being forced to follow are too restrictive and old fashioned. He will filibuster with the argument that "everyone else is doing it," and the real reason you won't let him do it is because you don't trust him and will never trust him; although so-and-so's parents trust him because they are letting him do it. Regardless of the argument that he presents, stick to your decision and explain to him that it would be much easier for you to give in to him and say yes, but that you love him enough to say no!

A young person striving for independence loves to be treated as an adult. Therefore, reward him when he makes a mature decision. A good way to do this is to grant him a "token" of more freedom. Be careful not to grant him more freedom than he is capable of handling. Find the balance of proper rewards for appropriate actions.

Kids & Television

In a subtle way, television, Hollywood, and movies are shaping the way our children view life and the world about them. Hollywood gives a child the impression that adultery, fornication, homosexuality, and violence are the norm, and even to be expected in life. The promiscuous lifestyle is depicted as the standard and the Christian lifestyle is portrayed as odd, weird, or strange. Marriage is often shown as a negative lifestyle rather than the "God ordained" lifestyle that it truly is. Even children's programs such as South Park and The Simpsons teach disrespect for authority. These programs give children the impression that their parents are stupid and not qualified to give their children proper direction in life.

Most parents do not understand the under current of philosophy that is behind the development of most movie themes in Hollywood. Parents are under the impression that the reason there are so many illicit sex, violent, and anti-family themes in movies is because of the money that these movies generate in the box-offices. Yet, in reality, it is a documented fact that wholesome movies generate far more money than the movies that are filled with violence and sex. So the question must be asked, if money is not the issue, then why are the "trashy" movies dominating the movie market? The answer is simple, yet frightening. The producers are predominantly anti-family, anti-God, and anti-Christian! They are selling their message "wholesale" to our children and tragically the parents are paying for them.

How can a parent expect his child who practically lives in front of a T.V. set to act any other way but violent, inconsiderate, promiscuous, and rebellious, when this is the message that is being delivered to him day after day. The tragedy is that many parents just sit back and let it happen in their home before their very eyes. They even use T. V. as a form of baby sitting to keep the children occupied while they are doing things that they want to do.

Other forms of child entertainment should also be monitored. Violent and adult themes are found in video games and even in comic books. It is a parent's responsibility to protect his child from this form of "evil" that is invading our homes.

Many parents are not very knowledgeable in the area of "technological entertainment" such as the internet, IM's, and e-mail. Yet, their children are involved with these everyday of their lives and are quite knowledgeable about them. These arenas greatly influence their lives. A good acid test for a parent is to compare the amount of time he spends with his child to the amount of time his child spends with the "technological media." The result of this survey will determine "who" or "what" is the real dominant influence in the child's life.

The Danger of Organized Sports

I would like to express a word of caution concerning "organized sports." What I mean by organized sports is not young people playing basketball in a gym, or young people playing football in the back yard, but sports that are structured in a public setting in such a way that all that counts is the "game" and "winning the game."

For many years I have taken a stand against "organized sports" for a number of reasons. One of the reasons is the "worldly environment" in which the sport is played. Another is the immense amount of time involved in not only playing the games, but also in the practices before the games. Many times this causes a child and his parents to miss church services or church functions. This gives the child the impression that sports are more important than God, church, and church activities. Another reason is the negative drawing effect that "organized sports" has on the child, by drawing him away from Christian thinking to worldly thinking. Another reason is the "out-of-balance" competitive attitude that is instilled into children and young people. They are often told by their coaches and others involved in the game, that all that counts in life is "winning the game."

I would also like to approach this subject from another direction without taking anything away from the "above mentioned reasons." A young person who becomes good at an organized sport often finds himself in the so-called "in-crowd" at school. He is looked upon as a very popular person. In fact, he is almost considered a hero, maybe even as a "demigod." Unfortunately, what makes him popular is not his love for God, family, or for his church. It is not his good attitude, or his academic achievements--just his ability to throw or catch a ball, or to be able to run faster than someone else.

This "hero mentality" follows him until he graduates. His whole world up until this point in time is not academics or real life issues, but sports. When he graduates, he suddenly finds himself in a void, unless he is good (as defined by the "sports world") enough to pursue his athletic skills in college. This often causes a young person to flounder and loose all sense of direction for his future.

I am not saying that "organized sports" have no positives. I know they provide much needed discipline for some children. I know they also teach young people to work as a team. But what I am saying is that the negatives greatly outweigh the positives, and the positives can be taught in numerous other ways outside of "organized sports."

Concerning Sexual Matters

When a child asks his parents questions concerning sexual matters, it is important that the parent not ignore him. It is amazing how many parents there are who are uncomfortable with this subject. However, just ignoring the questions concerning sex will not make them go away. Some parents try the "postponement method" by talking about a stork or a cabbage patch. This may actually work for a while, but at some point it will insult the child's intelligence. God created children to be curious, and their curiosity will be fulfilled in one way or another. A wise parent will take his child's questions seriously and answer him at his level of maturity.

Sex education is a parental responsibility. When hormones begin to flow, it is vital that children get the proper answers to the questions concerning the new things that are taking place in their body. When the appropriate time arises, a parent must teach his child the proper attitude toward sex. He must teach him that it is a wonderful gift given by God, but it is reserved only for the marriage bond. It is a parent's responsibility to do this. After all, the child will not get this point of view from friends, Hollywood, or secular school teachers, who will just teach sex education with moral guidelines. As a parent, we must step in ahead of the distorted information that the world will be pumping into our children's minds.

Many children have the impression that sex is something naughty. As a result, they will whisper and snicker to each other secretly about it. This is why, at the appropriate age, a parent should educate his child on the fact that God created sex, and that it is beautiful and good, but is reserved by God to be experienced by a man and woman within the bonds of matrimony.

The education of a child on the subject of sex is not a one time event. A parent must progressively educate his child as he moves through different levels of maturity in his life. When he is very young and expresses the first question of curiosity as to where he came from, the parent should answer his question in a basic, yet truthful form. There is a temptation at this point in a child's life for the parent to revert to the "stork" or to the "cabbage patch" answer. To overcome this temptation, keep in mind that a child will always be comfortable with the truth, as long as a parent is able to transpose the truth to the child's maturity level. Keep in mind that it is usually the parent who is uncomfortable with the subject of sex and not the child.

> **We must step in ahead of the distorted information that the world will be pumping into our children's minds.**

As a child grows older, if a parent will be open with him on this subject, he will come to the parent with further questions rather than try to get them answered elsewhere. Most of the distorted and vulgar concepts about sex come from children trying to gain knowledge about the "facts of life" from places such as secular schools,

177

peers, and Hollywood. When Mom or Dad evades the subject, their children are left with no other choice but to seek their answers from these sources.

When the time comes to talk to your child about the subject of sex, remember that children tend to be open about discussing with others any subject that they have been learning about. For this reason, it is also important that a parent explain to his child that the subject of sex is so special in the eyes of God that it should only be discussed at home with the people that he loves. This reminds me of a comic caption of Charlie Brown that I saw years ago in a newspaper. Mr. and Mrs. Smith were visiting Charlie Brown's parents. Charlie Brown walked into the living room and started staring at Mrs. Smith's dress. She looked at Charlie Brown and said, "Charlie Brown, I see you are staring at my dress. Do you like it?" Charlie Brown replied, "No M'am! I am just surprised that you are wearing a dress!" Mrs. Smith then asked, "Why, Charlie Brown, what would make you say that?" He answered, "Well, my dad is always saying that you are the one who wears the pants in your family."

Dealing With Loneliness

Statistics tell us that one of the top causes of suicidal thoughts in teenagers is a result of feelings of extreme isolation. It is very important for a parent to get the message across to his child that he is never alone. All children, especially teenagers, go through periods of time when they feel lonely, misunderstood, or rejected. This is a natural part of a child growing to maturity. These feelings will normally pass away, as a new set of circumstances replace the old ones. However, there are times when these negative feelings "go to seed." If a parent has a good relationship with his child, he will be able to step in at this point and steer his child through these troubling times by letting him know that he is there for him.

Oftentimes, there is a direct correlation between the feelings of loneliness, emptiness, and isolation that the child is having, and the set of circumstances that the child is experiencing. If a parent will take the time to help his child work through or change the circumstances that he is in, usually the feelings of isolation will decrease or even disappear. For example, if a young person's loneliness and isolation is stemming from the feeling of being under pressure from having too many things to do, the problem is usually a lack of prioritization in conjunction with poor time management. The solution in this case is to help the child learn to manage and prioritize his tasks in a timely way. The pressure on his life will diminish and usually the feelings of isolation will also diminish proportionally. This would seem to be such a simple solution which most parents would think their child could figure out on his own. What many parents fail to realize is that problems can be so overwhelming to the immature mind of a child that it can easily overpower him. It is in this emotional state that a child's feelings are telling him that no one understands or truly cares about what he is going through.

When a child tells his parent that no one understands him, it will do the parent no good to try and convince the child that he does understand. The best response the parent can give the child in this situation is to say something like, "I know I don't understand what you are going through, but I would sure like to understand better if you will help me." Usually this type of approach by the parent will begin to unveil the underlying problem or problems that are creating the feelings of isolation and loneliness in the child.

In the previously-mentioned example, the problem was not loneliness and isolation. That was the resulting symptoms of the problem which the child was feeling. The root of the problem was prioritization and time management. Once the source of the problem was identified and dealt with, the symptoms disappeared.

Chapter 9
Building Your Child's Future

Play to Their Strengths

Motivation is a factor that will greatly determine the future of your child. A child will not excel as he matures if he is not first motivated to do so. To a certain degree, a child may motivate himself and there are even some rare occurrences when a child may completely motivate himself. But for the most part, motivation is an on-going process that is produced by the parents of the child, and to a lesser degree by teachers and mentors in the child's life.

Children tend to be motivated more in some areas than in others. As a child matures, it is the parent's responsibility to move his child in the direction of his strengths. For example, my son, Jared, from a small boy has been mechanically inclined. From the young age of four years old, I can remember Jared taking toys apart just to see what made them work. He did not do this in a destructive way, in fact, most of the time he would get them back together with little or no outside help. As he became

181

a young teenager, he would read manuals on electronic and mechanical devices and absorb, not only how to use them, but the theory involved in how they worked. As Beverly and I saw this talent unfold, we gradually encouraged Jared to continue in this direction, always playing to his strengths and talents. No wonder, that Jared has earned a degree in Mechanical Engineering from Louisiana Tech University. By the way, I have to be honest, there may have been a bit of a selfish motive on my part in pushing Jared in this direction. I discovered a number of years ago that if I couldn't figure out how some device worked, I could just ask him.

The Lord has placed within every child unique gifts and talents. It is a parent's responsibility to identify his child's area of competence and move him in that direction. For one, it will be music; for another, it will be math, speech, writing, mechanics, and the list goes on and on. By moving a child toward the area of his competence, a parent is helping him play to his strengths. After he has been involved in the area of his strengths for a while, he will feel good about himself and about life in general.

If a child is coasting through life with an attitude of "I don't care," the problem could be that he has never been encouraged to excel in his area of giftedness. In other words, no one has ever taken the time to point out to him his strengths and talents. The thing for a parent to do is to first identify the child's areas of strength and move him in that direction. This will make him look at life from a totally different viewpoint. Instead of having the attitude of "I can't do anything right, so why try," he will have the attitude of "I can do this well, so I probably can do other things well also."

A child is strongly motivated by his desire. If a parent invests his time in steering his child's desire in the right direction, he is going a long way in determining his child's future. A parent must be very careful to be honest with himself in this area. He must never allow his personal desires to get in the way. Some parents make the mistake of trying to re-live their life through their children. Doing so will limit a child's potential and will prevent him from becoming all that he can be upon maturity.

A parent must determine his child's strengths and weaknesses and then gently coax the child to develop his strengths. This will, to a degree develop into an ongoing process. As he is gradually encouraged to move in the direction of his strengths, and he gets a few wins under his belt, the momentum caused by this will create desire. When a child feels good about what he has accomplished, he naturally will feel good about himself. This in turn motivates him to move further in the direction of what makes him feel good about himself. To a degree, this becomes a positive, self-perpetuating cycle.

Every child is "fearfully and wonderfully made" by God. Each has his own unique personality. Do not make the mistake of comparing your children one to another; or to other children outside of your immediate family. Each child responds to a situation in his own distinctive way. Therefore, a parent must deal with his child in the unique way that matches his personality make-up.

Seeing the Big Picture

As we work at building-up our children we must always see the "big picture." Don't get hung up on isolated issues, but be broad minded enough to always see the final objective, and that is to develop a well balanced, mature, and virtuous child. As the old saying goes, "It is not whether we win or lose individual battles, but whether we win the war." Therefore choose your battles carefully because some of them are not worth the fight. Just as someone once said, "Every man is big enough to skin a skunk, but sometimes it is just not worth the stink."

As a parent, there will be times, no matter how hard you try, when situations will not be right for your child. During these times you must focus on the big picture. If your child is doing better today than he was a year or two ago, then you are gradually "winning the war."

Rearing children is analogous to what the Lord told Moses concerning the Promised Land that the Children of Israel were about to enter into:

> *But the land, whither ye go to possess it, is a land of hills and valleys, and drinketh water of the rain of heaven.*
> *(Deuteronomy 11:11)*

As parents, we realize that life is composed of ups and downs (hills and valleys). Our goal is to make every hill experience a little higher than the one before; all the while keeping in mind that it takes a valley to make any two hills. So it is with our children. We cannot lose focus when our child is going through a troubling time. Knowing that if we will be consistently committed to building them up, our efforts will eventually be rewarded by seeing them on the top of the next hill.

Another facet of seeing the big picture is remembering that we, as parents, are seeing a situation with the perception of an adult, and our children are seeing the same situation with the perception of a child. Often, the parent and child will see the same situation and come to two different conclusions. The reason this happens is that the child processes the situation at the mental and emotional level of a child or teenager. It is all a matter of perception. A parent must bear this in mind as he communicates with his child.

Perhaps the most important area involved with seeing the big picture is identifying the weaknesses that result from our child's personality mixture. If we identify these glitches and work on them while the child is young, it can prevent fatal character flaws in our child's future. A little flaw in a child is analogous to a lion cub growing into an adult lion. If the cub is not conquered while it is young, it will grow into a lion with the potential of immense destruction. The scripture tells us in Proverbs 4:26 that we should ponder the path of our feet and that by doing so, our "ways" will be established. In like manner, if a parent will identify the little weaknesses in his child while he is young, he can deal with them before they cause him to be thrown completely off-course as he grows older.

Teach Them to Look Beyond the Moment

This is the age of instant gratification. One of the hardest things for a child to do is to learn to wait. A parent must teach his child to set goals in life, and then have the patience to see them come to fruition.

For most children, their greatest goals in life are to hear the dismissal bells at the end of the school day so they can go to the mall with their friends. They live only for the moment. Children tend to have a short attention span. It is a parent's responsibility to get the child to look beyond the moment. To do this, he must be encouraged to consider what he wants to accomplish in life.

A child must be educated to the fact that some things don't happen instantly. He must set goals in life and then learn to patiently reach for them. In other words, he must learn that many of the best things in life take time to acquire. To get them, he must set his goals for them, work toward them, and in the meantime, patiently wait for them.

Teach Them to Make Good Choices

A parent must teach his child the importance of making good choices in life. Prior to the age of three, or possibly four, most of a child's choices are made by his parents. The type of baby bed he will sleep in, the color of his car seat, the kind of food he is allowed to eat, the type of toys that are purchased for him, the brand of clothes he wears, and on and on it could go.

Choice is of vital importance in a child's life, and will continue to be important from his childhood to the day that he passes from this life. The scripture instructs us in Joshua 24:15 to "Choose you this day whom ye will serve." The Word of God also says in Isaiah 7:15 that we are to "Refuse the evil, and choose the good."

Options increase as a child grows older. Most choices for a young child come to him in the form of commands: "Don't fight with your sister!" "Go to Bed!" "Don't pull the dog's tail!" "Don't climb on that table!" He makes the active choice as to whether he will obey the command or not and then faces the consequences of his decision. As the child grows older, his options increase exponentially. If he is not taught from a young age, to make his choices wisely, he will become overwhelmed by them.

> **Sound judgment and the weighing out of options is something that only comes through time and experience.**

I have observed some parents who have exercised too much restraint on their children. Rather than guiding their child through the process of making wise choices in life, they restrained them and controlled them to the point that they had very little opportunity to make their own decisions about their future. The young people who were reared under these circumstances, once released into the real world, did not have a clue as to how to make wise and prudent decisions on their own.

The exercising of sound judgment and the weighing out of options is something that comes to a child through time and experience. Many parents get the idea that age alone is the criteria that qualifies a child to make decisions in life. Certainly age should play a part in deciding whether a child is allowed to make his own decisions concerning certain matters. For example, a three year old child is not qualified to make the decision as to whether he will play with a loaded pistol or not. At the same time, a seventeen year old child should be allowed to make the decision as to whether he wants to go deer hunting with his older brother. Once a child is of an age to make a decision, a parent should guide him through the steps of making his own choice in matters for which he is qualified, and then release him to do so. This will provide him with the experience that he will need to make appropriate choices in other matters that will come his way after he leaves home and is on his on.

As a child is released to make more and more decisions, keep in mind that some of his decisions will not be perfect. In fact, some will be totally wrong. Yet, even these decisions will provide the experience that he will need to make wiser ones in the future.

Because of a child's limited experience, he may be very narrow in his vision and perception of a situation and may not know that other options exist. The responsibility of a parent in this situation is to open his mind to the other options that exist, but at the same time, not make the decision for him. When most children are shown better options, more often than not, they will choose the best option on their own.

While on the subject of choices, a parent must let his child know that there are two very important choices that he will make in life. They are as follows: First and most importantly, he must choose whether he is going to live for God or not. Next in importance, he will choose the spouse with whom he will live for the rest of his life with. This person will add value and compliment his life or, on the other hand, will take away from, and limit his life. On these two choices hinge his future in this life and, to a great degree, his future in Eternal Life.

Ready for Every Age Level

Make sure your child is ready for every age level of life. Part of building his future is thinking ahead for him and preparing him for every stage of life that will inevitably come his way. Each stage of life has its own unique challenges, whether it is young childhood, adolescence, or young adulthood.

Some parents live in denial. They refuse to believe that their children will ever grow up. For this reason, they do not make their child accountable for his actions. I remember one child in the church that I pastor who did things that were termed "cute" when he was a toddler. He would run up to people and grab them by the leg. As he got older he continued doing the same thing. I have seen him run up to elderly church members and almost knock them over. I overheard one of them say, "That's just not cute anymore." Unfortunately, his parents still think it's cute because in their mind they still look at him as a toddler. The same problem of denial is revealed in the way that some parents allow their children to dress. These parents would think it unacceptable for a woman to wear a mini-skirt, yet they will allow their fourteen or fifteen year old daughter to wear a dress five or six inches above her knees and will pass it off thinking that she is but a child. Of course reality hits when their child is having a child.

Socially Functioning Kids

This is an age of "high-tech" video games and the internet. In fact, the children of this generation are called the "Net Generation." For this reason, a parent has the responsibility of watching carefully to make sure that the social side of his child is developing properly. A child who spends most of his discretionary time playing video games and "surfing the net" can easily become socially dysfunctional. The tendency of a child toward becoming a loner during his adolescent years will greatly magnify itself after he becomes a teenager. This is also the time in his life when it is most important that he be accepted by his peer group. For this reason, as a parent, you must set limits on how much time your child spends with these "high tech" gadgets.

As a parent, encourage your child to socialize. Encourage him to invite his friends home to visit with him. Guide him in the proper ways of interacting with others. Take him to outings and socials where there are other young boys and girls of his age. It is vital that a child socially interacts with his peer group. Notice what the scripture says on this subject:

> *Iron sharpeneth iron; so a man sharpeneth the countenance of his friend.*
> *(Proverbs 27:17)*

This applies to children as well as to adults. When children rub shoulders with one another, the rough edges are rubbed off of their personalities and they are taught how to give, take and share. Your child's ability to properly cope with life in the future is, in many ways dependant upon his ability to create and maintain relationships with his peers at a young age. His relationship with others such as his spouse, friends, employers, and members of his church will be greatly affected by his social functionality.

Say Goodbye to Your Old Lifestyle

When a person chooses to become a parent, he is forfeiting his old lifestyle. That is, if he plans to become a good parent. To build his child's future, a parent must be willing to say goodbye to his past.

A number of years ago, the associate pastor of our church, Ricky and his wife Mona, were preparing to have their first child. Ricky is on the high end of being sanguine in personality. About a month prior to the birth of Trevor, Ricky came to me and with a smirk on his face said, "Mona and I discussed this baby situation and we have decided that this 'New baby in the House thing' is not going to change our lifestyle." Of course, being the highly confidential pastor that I am, I informed the entire church from behind the pulpit, that Ricky and Mona said that a new baby in the house was not going to change their lifestyle. For months after Trevor was born, people in the church were still asking Ricky whether the new baby had changed his and Mona's lifestyle. Ricky would jokingly answer back, "Oh, not at all."

As a parent, we must recognize that we must make the sacrifice of changing the comforts of our old "pre-parent" lifestyle and use the time and energy that we once gave to ourselves, to building character, values, principles, and virtue in our children.

I cannot recall all of the countless times that Beverly has carted our children and their friends over all of God's creation without any regard to her personal needs being met. When Beverly and I had to make the choice of our getting new clothes, or the children having new clothes, you can just guess who got them. When I wanted to eat at a steakhouse (the few times we could afford it while the children were young) and Corrie, Jared, and Layna wanted to eat at McDonalds, it is quite obvious where we ate. You know, those French fries weren't so bad once your taste buds became "immune" to them. That was quite a few hundred "happy meals" later.

It takes a sacrifice of time, energy, money, and personal comfort to properly build-up children in the way that God wants them to go.

Hold Them While You Let Them Go

Well, it finally happened. Beverly and I recently saw our last child graduate college. She is now engaged to be married. What a strange set of emotions went though our mind and heart that day as we watched Layna walk across the platform and receive her diploma. The only consolation is that she would be moving back home for a while.

As parents, a chapter in our lives closed that day. When Beverly and I got home and stepped into our house, we knew that life would be forever changed for us. Of course, the feeling did not last long. When the weekends come, the kids often all come visit, and everything is back to its hectic, normal pace. The telephone rings unceasingly, music blares, friends ring the doorbell, the grandkids are chattering about, the washer are dryer are in use almost twenty-four hours a day, and I could go on and on. This is exactly the way it should be.

As parents, we must never forget the fact that our goal is to produce independence in our children. In fact, the word of God identifies independence as the Biblical outcome of parenting:

> *And he answered and said unto them, Have ye not read, that he which made them at the beginning made them male and female, And said, For this cause shall a man leave father and mother, and shall cleave to his wife: and they twain shall be one flesh?*
>
> *(Matthew 19:4-5)*

Notice, the scripture says "a man shall leave his mother and father". This is the definitive goal that a parent should have in mind as he rears his children. I read an outstanding book many years age. It was entitled, Hold Me While You Let Me Go. It is a book that I would encourage any parent to read, especially if they are having trouble with releasing their children. The title says everything. We are to love our children and hold them tightly in our hearts throughout their lifetime, even after they are married and gone. At the same time, our goal is to release them as they mature, to become independent, productive adults.

Often, a parent subconsciously tries to prevent his child from moving toward independence. It is a parent's nature to be protective and if he is not careful, he will tend to become over-protective just at the time when he should begin to release his child. To counter this, a parent must make a conscious effort to move through the process of releasing his child, within the framework of proper timing, and in accordance with the circumstances involved. This will allow a parent to monitor his child's progress as he moves toward independence. At this point, the child is still young enough to receive correction or redirection, depending on the circumstances.

It is at this time in a child's life, that a parent must wear two different hats. One is the hat of a loving, yet correcting parent. The other is the hat of a friend that is standing at a distance, encouraging his child, yet not controlling him. There is a reason for the dual role of a parent at this stage in the child's life. It is at this phase of life that a child is vacillating between child-like and adult thoughts, feelings, and attitudes. During this period of the child's life, the parent must do the old "juggling act." He must change "hats" from parent to friend and back to parent, depending on the circumstances. For example, if a parent were to wear his "parent hat" while his child is in the adult mode, it can cause his child to be embarrassed or humiliated. On the other hand, if a parent wears his "friend hat" when his child is in the child mode, and in need of direction and guidance, it can lead to precarious or serious problems.

> As parents, we must never forget the fact that our goal is to produce independence in our children.

The Imperfect Parent

In a survey taken across The United States, a few years ago, American children were asked, "What words do you want most to come out of your parent's mouths?" The overwhelming "first place" answer was, "I love you." Now what's really interesting and also very important for parents to know, is the "second place" answer which was, "I am sorry, I was wrong."

As you approach the end of this book, it is important that you remember that no parent is perfect. All parents will make mistakes in parenting their children. Some parents have the idea that it is wrong to admit to their children that they have made mistakes. They have the misconceived idea that it is inappropriate to display vulnerability to their children. In reality, just the opposite is the case. It is vital to the well being of a child to know that his parents do make mistakes, just as he does, and that they are willing to own up to them. It releases him to take appropriate risks in life, knowing from the example of his parents that to "err" and ask forgiveness is part of being human.

A child that sees his mom or dad model the concept of owning up to their mistakes usually becomes a secure and balanced child. As this child grows into adulthood, he will usually carry far less emotional baggage with him than a child who hasn't been mentored by his parents in the areas of admitting mistakes and asking forgiveness for them.

Keep in mind, that children are not stupid. In fact, they are much smarter than we give them credit for. They know, just from observation, that their parents make mistakes; in fact, many mistakes. They then relate the attitude of a parent who refuses to admit or own up to his mistakes to a form of hypocrisy. The end result of this is that the parent, instead of modeling vulnerability and honesty, is modeling hypocrisy and deception.

This same concept goes far deeper than the parent-child relationship. It has strong Spiritual meaning. If a parent has never modeled asking forgiveness, how will he ever lead his child to the Lord? The first step toward salvation is repentance. That is when we admit that we are a sinner and ask God for forgiveness. How can a child take this first step toward his Heavenly Father, if he has not been mentored in this step by his earthly father?

In a parent, proper parenting begins with a proper attitude. A parent is a composite of the experiences of his past. The areas of his life that he has conquered or failed to conquer, quickly show themselves when he begins to exercise his role as a parent. For example, if a parent has not learned to control his temper, he will be quick to respond in anger toward the actions of his children. Another example is in the area of self-esteem. If a parent has not conquered low self-esteem in his personal life, he will then be incapable of thinking highly of his children. This, in turn, will then re-create the pattern of low self-esteem in his children. Good parenting does not begin with good parenting techniques, but with a parent having a good attitude about himself.

> **Proper parenting begins with a proper attitude.**

I now come to the close of this book with this admonition. As a parent, I encourage you to be committed to personal excellence. Just as you strive to upgrade yourself in your career skills so that you may perform better on your job resulting in higher positions and a better salary, so should you strive to become a better and more efficient parent. Read parenting books, such as this one. Go to seminars on how to improve your parenting skills. Listen to constructive criticism from your friends. This does not mean that you have to follow all of their advice. Yet, keep in mind that sometimes they will see things that need attention in your actions and attitude toward your children that you can not see on your own.

Remember, your kids are under construction and you are the key "builder" in their life. I pray that the Lord will help you to become a "Master builder." May He bless and help you as you work at building great kids.